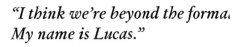

"I think we're beyond the forma...
My name is Lucas."

Lucy bit her lip.

He groaned.

"I understand that you agreed to sing for my grandfather's wake, and I feel bad that I didn't even know that you could sing, but I have to know something."

"Mr. Dear—" She put her hand up in front of her and closed her eyes. "Lucas, I…" she shook her head, her eyes unable to meet his.

He placed his crooked finger beneath her chin and lifted her face so he could see her clearly.

What are you doing, Deardon?

Alarm bells sounded in his head and he swallowed the lump that had formed in his throat. His heart pounded in his ears, his jaw flexed, and everything inside of him told him he should step back, but he could not make himself pull his hand away from her.

"Tell me you don't want to get married." The intoxicating scent of citrus infused in her hair filled his nostrils as a light breeze worked through the house, blowing her tresses in wisps in front of him. "Tell me you dream of running away and singing on a big, fancy stage." He captured her hand and pinned it to his chest. "Tell me you don't think about me. Tell me you don't want me," he pleaded, "and I will leave for Oregon tomorrow and you will never see me again."

Painstaking silence.

"I can't tell you any of those things," she finally whispered.

Damn.

LUCAS

DEARDON MINI-SERIES, BOOK TWO

KELLI ANN MORGAN

inspire books

Inspire Books
A Division of Inspire Creative Services
937 West 1350 North, Clinton, Utah 84015, USA

LUCAS

An Inspire Book published by arrangement with the author

First Inspire Books paperback edition April, 2015

ISBN-13: 978-1-939049-19-3
ISBN-10: 1939049199

Printed in the United States of America

PRAISE FOR THE NOVELS OF
BESTSELLING AUTHOR

KELLI ANN MORGAN

"This is a great romance story teller. Ms. Morgan really know how to write about the west in a very engaging way. History comes alive. And her characters are interesting. The romance is chemistry laden and smoldering. But, manages to still be clean."

—*CiCi J.* on THE IRON HORSEMAN

"There is a mystery to be solved...a fortune to be found and a love story interwoven to make a very entertaining book..."

—*Karen W.* on THE BLACKSMITH

"There were many twists and turns. This book has mystery, suspense, love, danger, and laughter. I thoroughly enjoyed."

—*Annette K. Hernandez* on THE BOUNTY HUNTER

"Well written adventure romance with the flavor of a Louis L'Amour."

—*Beth Smoot* on THE RANCHER

"I love mail-order bride books. It speaks to me of women with great strength and courage to travel and marry a stranger. This story is so special that I read it in one day. It definitely is a book to read any day of the week or season. It had just the right balance of romance and intrigue. It was something believable. Ms. Kelli Ann Morgan is an excellent story teller."

—*Linda M.* on JONAH

ACKNOWLEDGEMENTS

To my wonderful friends and fellow writers who plan and host our Crazy Ivans and special writing retreats where I am continually inspired and replenished.

To my amazing beta readers, Rocky Palmer, Jen Morgan, and Jen Sisneros! I can't express enough my gratitude for your willingness to be extra sets of eyes and for the additional insights you provided. THANK YOU!

And to Grant, the love of my life, and very talented alpha reader—your brutal honesty, constructive criticism, and push for me to write the best stories possible are invaluable. I love you and am so grateful for your continued support and encouragement. You're AMAZING!

*To my sisters, Kathy and Cheri,
for being two of my biggest fans.
The old adage applies—
sisters by chance, friends by choice.*

LUCAS

DEARDON MINI-SERIES, BOOK TWO

CHAPTER ONE

Oregon, October 1861

"How in the hell did you do that?"

Lucas Deardon's shoulder sat at an odd angle as he met his brother's concern with an unabashed grin. He'd never outright lied to Jonah before and he wasn't about to start now.

"Breaking the bronc over at the Wilson place."

Jonah froze, then turned away from him, his hands balled into fists. "And to think I was worried you'd been trying to impress the hands with all of those fancy rodeo circus tricks of yours." He finished wrapping the rope he held around his arm and draped it over one of the fence posts. "I thought we'd agreed. No wild horses." His voice was quiet, not at all what Lucas had expected. He picked up the tool crate and headed toward the barn.

A thread of guilt wove its way through Lucas's gut. But there was something about working with the wild horses that made Lucas feel close to his brother, Henry. Things around the ranch had not been the same since the accident and they'd all struggled to find their place and fill the hole his eldest brother had left behind.

"I'm not Henry, Jonah."

Henry had had talent in spades, especially when it came to breaking horses, and Lucas had always looked up to him. But he was his own man and it was time Jonah realized that.

Jonah whipped around, jostling the tools in the crate.

"No, you're not Henry." His eyebrows scrunched together, his eyes squinted. "Henry's dead!" he yelled. Then, as quickly as he'd raised his voice, he softened and turned back for the barn.

Lucas caught up to him.

"I would have thought you'd have learned from his mistake. You don't have anything to prove." When Jonah reached the barn door, he set the crate down and slid it open.

"What happened to Henry was an accident. Accidents happen, but living in fear of what *could* happen isn't living, big brother."

Jonah retrieved the tools and returned them to the worktable inside the barn. He placed his hands, shoulder width apart, on the flat surface and dropped his head.

"And, I have everything to prove."

"To who?" Jonah turned to look at him. "Not to Dad, and certainly not to me." He pushed past Lucas, waiting for him to follow, then slid the barn door closed behind him. Without missing a step, he ventured toward the stables.

Lucas followed, still holding his injured arm. "To all of you. And to myself. I'm not a kid anymore, Jonah. I see what you do around here to keep us afloat and I want to help. I work hard around here, but I could be doing so much more."

"Here," Jonah pulled one of the horseshoes from a nail in the wall and held it out, "take this."

Lucas reached out to take it.

"With your other hand."

"But—"

"Open your hand, curl your fingers around the metal, and just hold it down at your side."

He's got to be joking.

Lucas opened his fingers with some effort. What had been a dull ache a few moments ago was growing more painful by the moment and the swelling of his shoulder strained against the seams of his shirt sleeve.

Jonah placed the toe of the horseshoe in Lucas's hand.

"Are you trying to kill me?" Lucas asked with disbelief.

Jonah added another horseshoe. And another, until Lucas's arm felt like it might come apart.

POP!

Lucas rotated his arm in awe. "How did you know to do that?"

"Remember right after Mama left...?" His older brother looked up at him, then shook his head. "Never mind, kid. You were only, what, seven years old? Let's just say it's an old family trick."

Lucas didn't want to think about the woman who'd abandoned their family. He remembered her beautiful voice and ability to sing, but those talents had been more important to her than her own children. It had taken a long time for him to understand that there was nothing he could have done to make her stay. He'd learned to be happy without her.

"I remember she left. That's enough," Lucas told him.

"How'd he take it?" Noah, the brother just older than Lucas, popped his head into the stable as if not keen on exposing his entire body to Jonah's anticipated ire.

"You knew?" Jonah asked accusingly.

"Look at this." Lucas flapped his arm up and down like it was a chicken wing.

Ouch. He stopped.

Noah's eyes widened. "That's pretty good, doc," he teased as he stood up straight and walked fully into the barn, inspecting Lucas's arm. "Hey," he said as he turned back to Jonah, "Dad wants to see us in the house. All of us." He looked at Lucas. "Said it was important."

Lucas returned the horseshoes gingerly to the rack on the wall. His shoulder hurt, but at least the mounting pressure had been relieved when it popped back into place. He flexed his hand, stretching his fingers, as he slipped out the door ahead of Jonah and caught up to Noah, who nudged him playfully.

"See. No harm done," he whispered.

"Easy for you to say." Lucas rubbed the offending spot on his shoulder and flexed his hand again. "It might be a while before I can hold the reins tight enough to stay on that bronc. He sure is a beaut, but it'll take a bit more work before he's ready to ride."

Gabe Deardon wore scrunched brows as he sat behind the oversized desk in his den. He looked up at each of his sons as they entered the room. An odd, heavy cloud, almost thick enough to touch, loomed over them as they sat down. Lucas eased into the tall leatherback, careful to avoid contact with his tender shoulder.

When Jonah joined them, he closed the door and moved to sit on the arm of Lucas's chair.

"I'm just going to cut right to it," their father said, standing up from his seat. "Now that the telegraph has been completed and extends across the nation, the Pony Express will no longer be in service. They'll be closing their doors next week, I'm told."

A rock dropped inside Lucas's belly at the news. "What about our contract?"

"We knew it was only going to be a matter of time, son. However, they will pay us the remainder of what is due for this last run, but no more." His father moved around to the front of his desk and sat down, his ankles and arms crossed in front of him. "So, we have some hard decisions to make."

This was the first time Lucas had been invited to a

meeting that concerned anything to do with the ranch and was grateful his father saw him as man enough to be a part of the decision making going forward.

"We've stocked enough food and supplies to make it through this winter, but come spring, if we don't find another buyer, we'll be finished." Jonah moved into the chair next to Lucas.

"There may be another way to save the ranch." Their father met each one of them in the eyes. "But it will require a new mindset for all of us."

"What is it?" Noah asked, now sitting closer to the edge of his chair.

"Cattle."

Lucas glanced at his brothers who looked as dumbfounded as he felt.

"Cattle," Noah repeated.

"Cattle?" Jonah asked.

Gabe nodded. "Do you remember the Markhams?"

"The cattle rancher from Eureka?" Lucas didn't remember the rancher so much as his daughter, Clara. He smiled, despite himself.

Their father nodded. "He's decided to give up ranching all together and is moving his family back East."

"What does that have to do with us?" Jonah asked. "We're not planning a move to Eureka?"

"Certainly not. Markham approached me earlier this week and has offered to sell me his business and livestock for a third of the going price. Except for a few prized bulls. He already has someone lined up to buy his place, but they didn't want the herd, they want to farm the land."

"Why would he sell them to us? Wouldn't he be able to get full price at auction?" Lucas asked.

"For reasons that are his own, he wants to be in Augusta, Maine, by Christmas. And I'm not going to look a gift horse in the mouth."

"But we don't know anything about cattle ranching." Noah shoved his hands through his hair, then sat back against the chair.

Gabe leaned forward with a smile. "That's why he's offered to hire one of you to go and work the cattle with his foreman for the next few weeks to learn everything you can about the work. He'll pay a fair wage and offered to throw in one of his prized bulls as incentive."

As much as his father tried to mask his concern, Lucas could see the worry in his eyes. He was hiding something.

"What's the problem?" Jonah looked up at Gabe and asked what Lucas had been thinking. "You wouldn't be so concerned if it was going to be that easy?"

Their father laughed, something that Lucas hadn't heard very often—especially as of late.

"You know me all too well, son. We are in a bit of a predicament." He scratched the stubble on his neck with the back of his hand, then stood up to pace the room. "Money. I'm afraid we don't have enough on hand to even cover half of his asking price. Now that Lucas is injured," he nodded at his youngest son, "we've run out of options."

Lucas shot a glance at his brother, eyes wide.

"Wait," Jonah said, now rising to his feet, "you knew that Lucas was breaking horses for the Wilsons and you didn't tell me?"

Gabe's brows knitted together as his eyes flitted between Jonah and Lucas. "What are you talking about? I was referring to him reeling in the crowds at the Moonlight event next week with his fancy trick riding. I was sure he'd be able to sit on that bull longer than any of the others crazy enough to try."

Damn.

Lucas hadn't wanted Jonah to find out this way.

Jonah looked down at his feet, his hands clenched into fists. He took a deep breath.

"Jonah." Lucas stood to talk to his brother, to plead with him to understand, but when their eyes locked, it wasn't anger he saw, but sadness.

"I can't listen to this." He threw his hands up into the air, shaking his head. "You're going to get yourself killed and then where will we be?"

"Now, don't be such a woman," their father said mockingly.

Lucas held his breath.

Jonah raised a brow and turned on the man. "You are a selfish coward. I'm sorry that Henry's death was such an inconvenience to you. And now, you're willing to sacrifice another son? Maybe it's time *you* found another way."

"That's not fair—"

"No! You treating us like nothing more than your hired hands after mama left is what's not fair. You keeping us from our grandparents out of some sense of misguided pride is what's not fair. You want to talk to me about fair?" Jonah marched to the door. "How is it fair that four young boys lost both of their parents on the same day? Mama, when she walked out on us and you when you gave up hope."

Lucas dared a glance at their father who stood with his back straight, his jaw clenched, and his face redder than a beet. He looked as if he could spit nails. It was the first time he could ever remember his father being speechless.

"I will not make the same mistake you did when you left your family behind," Jonah said quietly, "but I'll be damned if I keep my mouth shut any longer. You want to try cattle ranching, fine. If that is what we have to do to build a legacy for our families, we'll do it. But we'll find another way. I owe that to Emma and to our child." He turned away and walked from the room.

"Jonah," Lucas called after him.

Silence.

The tension in the room grew thick and the weight of it came to rest on Lucas's shoulders. Without a good arm to use breaking in wild horses or entertaining spectators atop a bull, he would be worthless in helping his family keep their home—whether they traded in horses or cattle.

We'll find another way.

"You have a lot of talent, Lucas," Noah said as if reading his thoughts. "It may take some time, but he'll come around." He stood and picked his hat from their father's desk.

"What's this?" Noah asked, pulling an unopened envelope from a collection of papers on their father's desk. Noah held it up and showed Lucas. It had been addressed to Jonah, Noah, and Lucas Deardon with fancy writing. The corners were bent and it looked as if it had been there for quite some time, but had yet to be opened.

"It's nothing." Their father snatched it back from Noah's hands and cleared his throat.

"It was addressed to us. Don't you think we should at least know who it's from?" Noah persisted.

"Just someone trying to stir up trouble. Let's leave it at that." The stern expression on their father's face said that was the end of it and they should not press it any further.

Noah bobbed his head with a reluctant nod, but Lucas was growing increasingly suspicious of their father. Though tempted to snatch it right out of his hands, he refrained, gripping the brim of his hat a might tighter instead.

"Well, that didn't go over like I'd imagined." Their father tucked the letter in his back pocket and continued as if there was nothing else to say. "We still need to figure out how we can come up with the money for the herd. Why don't you boys take some time tonight and think on it. We'll discuss it again tomorrow. We'll leave a legacy all right."

Lucas and Noah looked at each other.

"Did Jonah say, 'our child?'" Lucas asked.

It only took a moment before both of them scrambled out the door to find their older brother. Jonah's words about their father having left his family behind had sparked an idea in Lucas. There was a way to get the money, but he doubted anyone was going to like it.

Lucas thought of the conversation he'd had with his cousin, Raine, when they'd visited Redbourne Ranch last year in Kansas. Raine had told him that Granddad Deardon had provided an inheritance for all his grandchildren if they married before the age of twenty-five. Jonah had met the requirement when he and Emma wed and Lucas knew if he could convince their grandfather to uphold his end, they would have enough to purchase the herd and save the ranch. If not, he could always ask for a job.

There was just one thing left to do. Find their grandfather.

"Do you ever get the feeling we are more like business partners than his family?" Noah asked as they stepped outside into the brisk evening air. "Jonah was right, you know. Mama leaving left Dad a broken man. I'm not sure he even remembers how to be just a father, not the boss," he mused.

Lucas's thoughts turned to the woman who'd destroyed their once happy family so long ago. "Do you ever wonder what it would have been like if she hadn't left? Do you think that letter was from her?" Lucas wondered aloud.

Noah turned to look at him. "Come on, we've got Jonah to find and work to do." He haphazardly smacked Lucas on the shoulder.

Arggggg. He bit back a curse.

CHAPTER TWO

Montana, Dakota Territory

Lucy Russell stepped down off the stage, followed by two other young women who'd come west for the same reason. A husband.

The burley driver stood up on his very tall seat and tossed down several packages for some of the townsfolk, a few large trunks, and a gaggle of smaller bags from atop the coach, earning him exaggerated gasps from the other two soon-to-be-brides. It took a moment before he found hers, but the man, who'd allowed her to ride on his seat when the coach had become too stuffy, carefully handed down her lone, oversized carpet bag.

"Good luck to you, Miss Russell," the driver called as he tipped his hat and recaptured the reins.

She smiled and waved him goodbye. With a quick attempt at brushing the thin layer of dirt from her traveling dress, she looked up to face the little town of Thistleberry, Montana. It was the hometown of Gilroy Hearn, her betrothed—even though she'd never met the man. The settlement was a far cry from the busy streets of New York, but as she took a deep breath, she couldn't help the excitement this opportunity brought. She had a plan. And this is where she would make her home.

Several men and women had gathered around the stage and Lucy looked for any sign of the man who'd been described in her letters—average height and build with a thin mustache. Plenty of men looking on fit that description, but as she glanced toward each of them, none seemed to be there to collect her.

Maybe he's just running late. It was hard, after all, to predict the exact time a stage might arrive.

A rather large framed man with sunny blond hair picked up the enormous blue trunk that belonged to one of her traveling companions and slung it up onto his back, evoking a giggle from the girl that made Lucy's eyes roll. A young, nice looking man with a slight mustache walked toward her and suddenly her heart started beating heavily in her chest. She stood up straight, prepared to offer her hand.

He smiled at her, tipped his hat, and reached down for the brown riveted trunk she hadn't realized sat next to her feet. Her uneasy smile froze in place, her gaze quickly darting from man to man as they lined the street.

He's not coming.

"Excuse me, ma'am, but are you Miss Lucy Russell?"

She spun around with a smile, anxious to meet the man who belonged to the deep and rugged baritone voice.

"Hello," she said, annoyed at the slight crack in her voice. She certainly hadn't expected him to have white hair and a clean shaven face.

He's old enough to be my grandfather, she mused as she craned her neck to look up at the tall gentleman. *He's certainly not average…anything.*

With her back straight and her chin held high, she extended her hand. "Gilroy Hearn, I presume?"

The man cleared his throat, but instead of taking her hand, he took her bag.

"Liam Deardon, ma'am," he corrected, meeting her eyes straight on. "Now, here's the thing..." He scrubbed the back of his curled fingers across his leathery looking jaw line.

Her stomach dropped along with her hand.

"If you'll just come with me I can explain on the way." He threw her bag into the back of a buckboard waiting behind them in front of the General Store.

"On the way to where?"

"Home," Mr. Deardon announced. "Whisper Ridge Ranch." He held out a hand to help her into the wagon.

She lifted her skirt and slid her other hand into his, unsure what to make of the situation. "I don't understand. Where is Mr. Hearn?" She sat on the bench, determined to silence the alarm that sounded in her head.

The older gentleman gingerly pulled himself up onto the wagon seat next to her and collected the reins. "I'm afraid I've got some bad news." He looked straight ahead and snapped the leather straps in his hands. "Hi-yah!"

Oregon, One Week Later

"Montana isn't that far away. It's only a couple of hundred miles," Lucas told Jonah as he tightened the saddle strap on his horse. He winced slightly at the pain the motion shot through his shoulder. "Adonis here will get me there with no problems, won't you boy?" He patted the gelding's back.

The horse whinnied as if he'd understood every word.

Lucas laughed.

"You can't travel there alone."

"He won't have to," Noah stepped into the stable and pulled his tack down off the wall.

Lucas smiled. "And just how did you get out of heading over to Eureka and working Markham's ranch?"

"Oh, I didn't. I'm to report there first thing tomorrow. I was referring to Jonah. I think he could use some distance from this place. From Dad."

"And what about Emma?" Lucas asked.

"What about me?" As if on cue, Jonah's bride walked through the stable doors.

His brother's face lit up and he scooped his wife into his arms and kissed her smack on the mouth.

Lucas knew he should look away, but it was good to see Jonah happy. He deserved that.

"Good morning," Emma greeted them, a light blush staining her cheeks.

The one thing he regretted about leaving so soon was that his niece or nephew would likely be born before he would return.

"You look beautiful, Emma," he said, leaning down and kissing her on the cheek.

"We'll miss you around here, Lucas. Take care of yourself." She handed him a small knapsack. "Just a few things for your journey."

"Thank you kindly, ma'am."

Jonah's forehead wrinkled above the bridge of his nose.

"I'll be fine," Lucas told them. "I've taken a job accompanying the stage as far as Virginia City. It's good money, enough to get me to Thistleberry and back. I'll be home before you know it."

"Does Dad know where you're headed? He should be the one leaving for Montana to face his family. Not you.

Not with that shoulder." Lucas knew how difficult it must have been for Jonah to stand up to their father, but he'd said it had been good for the soul, though he still sensed some hostility between the two men.

"I told him about the job with the stage and he was fine with it." Lucas took a step toward Jonah, who mumbled something unintelligible under his breath.

"Look, we all have to do our part. Noah is going to Eureka to learn cattle ranching, you have to oversee this last herd and its delivery, and I...well, I have to find Granddad Deardon and persuade him to un-disinherit us. Is that even a word?"

"No," Noah shook his head with a snort.

Jonah opened his mouth as if he was going to say something, but Emma stepped in between them, looking up at her husband.

"I don't know where I would have been without my grandfather. He is the reason I have you." She smiled.

A light chill swept over Lucas and gooseflesh rippled his skin.

"Your father is a proud man, Jonah. What was it you said? You shouldn't be punished for his mistakes." Emma threaded her arms beneath Jonah's and leaned up against him. "Lucas is right. Finding your grandfather may be more important than you think. And it's not just about the money. You should get to know him. While you still have a chance."

Lucas beamed, grateful that someone understood why he had to go. "That's a wise woman you've got there, big brother."

Jonah sighed. He bent down and brushed his lips lightly over Emma's, then deepened the kiss. When he pulled away, he lingered on her eyes a moment, then turned to Lucas.

"Take this." He set Emma aside as he pulled something from his pocket and slid it into Lucas's hand before yanking him into a fierce embrace. "God speed, baby brother," he whispered. "God speed." With a quick pat on the back he turned and walked from the stables.

"Good luck, Lucas," Emma said as she stood up on the tips of her toes and placed a kiss on his cheek before hurrying to join her husband.

When Lucas opened his hand to reveal an old, oval-shaped, gold locket, his heart skipped a beat. He clicked it open. There was a photograph on each side—one of his granddad and the other his grandmother—the last before she died. Because of the strain between their father and his family, Gabe Deardon's children hadn't even been allowed to go to her funeral. Lucas snapped it shut and squeezed with a grateful upturn of his mouth. He didn't remember much about the woman, except that her hair had always seemed to smell of warm bread. He smiled wider.

"You ready?" Noah had finished packing his beautiful paint gelding.

"As I'll ever be." He placed the closed locket in his vest pocket and scooped up Adonis's reins.

He and Noah would be able to ride together for the better half of the day before the road would take them in separate directions. They led their horses out into the yard and mounted.

"Let's go."

CHAPTER THREE

Montana, Dakota Territory, November

"When do you expect Mr. Deardon to return?" The gangly man in a dark green bowler hat inquired with a slight wiggle of his nose as he tried to readjust how his spectacles sat just below its bridge.

Wisps of snow had begun to fall again and now swirled in flurries around the man's head. Truth was, Liam should have been back from Virginia City days ago and Lucy worried that he would get caught in the coming storm.

"I know you mean well, Mr. Tacy, but I'm afraid I do not have any more information for you. I will see to it that Mr. Deardon knows you stopped by." She moved to close the door, but the man stuck his head inside, startling her. She jumped backward with a quick intake of breath.

"It is a matter of the utmost importance."

Quickly collecting herself, she smiled at him with patience she didn't feel. "I understand. Thank you." She pushed on the door until he was forced to retract his head and it closed completely. She leaned against it and blew a stray lock of hair from her eyes. Taking over the running of this household seemed a better idea a month ago when she'd faced destitution on the street.

Where are you, Liam? The man had become like the grandfather she'd never known. He was a good man. She just hoped he wasn't freezing out there. She made a mental note to have the foreman bring in another bundle of firewood for the hearth. He'd be home soon. From the way he spoke of the annual and much celebrated Deardon Thanksgiving Day tournament and feast, he wouldn't miss it.

Knock. Knock.

Lucy shook her head and spun to open the door.

"I thought I told you..."

Her head motioned backward at the sight of the tall, dark-haired man with brilliant blue eyes who stared down at her. To her surprise, it was not the lanky young lawyer, but a stranger—though there was something oddly familiar about him. He was a beautiful man.

Stop that, Lucy Russell. She cleared her throat.

The stranger looked behind him.

"I'm guessing that was meant for him?" He pointed to the well-dressed man who lifted his foot from the mud puddle he'd just found in front of his little metal carriage and looked back at the house with a scowl.

Lucy giggled and waved. She couldn't help herself.

"I'm sorry to disturb you, ma'am," the stranger said, pulling her from her wicked thoughts, "but I was wondering if this is where I might find Mr. William Deardon."

"This is Mr. Deardon's residence. May I help you?"

"Will you please tell him that Lucas is here to speak with him?"

"Lucas?" She recognized the name and her heart nearly jumped from her chest.

"Lucas Deardon, ma'am. His grandson."

Oh, my.

She'd thought the other Deardon men were handsome, but nothing had prepared her for this Deardon man. Liam had recounted how he had written to his estranged son, Gabriel, just after she'd arrived with the hopes of reconnecting with him and his boys by inviting them to Whisper Ridge for the holidays. By the way Liam had spoken of his grandsons, she half expected Lucas to be a young boy of ten or twelve, not a grown man.

She just stared at him for a moment.

"Ma'am," he said, pulling her from her thoughts.

"Is your father with you? Your brothers?" she asked expectantly, stepping up onto her toes in an attempt to look behind him. That wasn't going to work. He had to measure at least six feet, if not more.

"No, ma'am." He fiddled with the hat in his hand. "I've come alone." He met her eyes, his jaw set—prepared for the worst. She'd seen that look before. On Liam. She wanted to invite him in, but worried about the propriety of it. Tillie, the family's cook was in town gathering last minute supplies for the feast. Nancy, the housekeeper, had already come and gone for the day. And now, Lucy was the only one left in the house.

The sound of an excited bark filled the otherwise quiet house.

She turned to see Brewster, a beautiful border collie bounding toward her from the kitchen.

"Lucy, are you in here? The snow is coming dow..." Alex, one of Liam's daughters-in-law, stopped short as she walked into the living area, her normally quaffed hair, sopping wet. Lucy marveled at how the woman could still look so beautiful.

Thank you, she offered silently at having another woman in the house.

"Oh, I didn't realize you had a guest." Alex moved to the archway into the parlor and leaned against it, raising an appreciative brow at the man.

Lucy narrowed her eyes in a warning. Alex and Mara, the

ladies of Whisper Ridge, had been trying to convince her that most men were not like Gilroy Hearn and she should give the marriage idea another thought. She wasn't against the notion, especially with someone who looked like this Mr. Deardon, but she wasn't in any hurry.

As Brewster reached her, she bent down to pet the dog, but he leapt past her, headed straight for Liam's grandson, and jumped up with his front paws onto the man's legs.

"Down, boy!" she called. "I'm so sorry, Mr. Deardon. Normally, he's much better behaved," she said, trying to keep the giggle from her voice as she coaxed the animal off of him. "Please, come in."

The last thing Lucas had expected was for a young, strikingly beautiful woman to answer his grandfather's door. The friendly pup had surprised him too. He dropped down onto his haunches, allowing the dog to lick the side of his face.

"Hahaha." A hearty laugh escaped, despite himself. He reached into his pocket, retrieved his last piece of jerky, and gave it to the pup. "What's his name?" he asked as he stood up, watching the dog prance into another room with the dried meat dangling from his mouth.

Lucas suddenly felt more at ease than he had a moment before.

"That would be, Brewster." The woman stood aside, motioning for him to walk inside the enormous house. She pointed toward a parlor room at the front. "You really shouldn't indulge him. He already thinks he owns the place."

The heavenly aroma of fresh baked bread and roasting meat induced visions of a warm home-cooked meal—something Lucas hadn't eaten in a month's time. He ignored the loud rumbling sound that churned in his belly as he shook off the chill and reached up to brush off the snowflakes accumulated on his coat, biting back the curse that threatened at the awkward movement.

Blasted shoulder. It had been nearly a month and the arm was still giving him problems. Pain had become an unwelcome part of his life. Most of the time it didn't bother him, but once in a while when he moved it just so, it protested in the form of sharp, stabbing pains. Today was his lucky day.

"Thank you, kindly," he said as he wiped his boots on the mat and stepped over the threshold. He removed his hat and nodded at the blond woman standing in the archway, who watched him carefully as he followed the younger woman to the couch in front of the window.

"I'm afraid Mr. Deardon is..." she cleared her throat and started again. "I'm afraid your...grandfather, is unavailable right now."

The blond woman's eyes opened wide and with an oddly conspiratorial smile, she moved into the room and extended her hand.

"Grandfather?" she eyed him speculatively. "You must be one of Gabe's boys."

Lucas stood and took her hand. "Yes, ma'am. The youngest." He wasn't sure what he was supposed to say. He'd rehearsed the speech to his granddad hundreds of times over the last few weeks, but hadn't as much as thought about anyone else.

"Lucas?"

He nodded.

"I don't know if you'll remember me, but I'm Alexandra. Alex," she clarified. "I'm married to your father's youngest brother, Sam."

He glanced over at the woman who'd answered the door and couldn't help but wonder if *she* was someone's wife.

"I'm sorry." He shook his head. "It is very nice to meet you, ma'am." He barely remembered his grandparents. And at home, neither he, nor his brothers, had been allowed to talk about any of their extended family—except for Aunt Leah, of course, who wouldn't have let his father cut her out if he'd tried.

"Well, that's all right, dear." She turned to the other. "He certainly has the good manners of any Deardon I've known or raised." With a smile, she looked back at him. "I'm sure the next few days will offer the opportunity for us to get reacquainted."

"I hope so, ma'am." Lucas nodded.

"Aunt Alex," she corrected with a smile. "Well, I think you'll fit in just fine around here," she said with a satisfied nod. "You're only a little older than a couple of our boys. They'll show you around," she said with a satisfied nod. "Now, I'm sure Lucy will see to it that you are taken care of until your granddad returns." She turned her attention to the woman standing beside him. "Any word?"

"Not yet."

Alex nodded. "Well, maybe we should keep you a secret. For now," she added with a little twinkle in her eye. "I'd hate for Liam to think I'd stolen his surprise. I'm just going to grab some sugar to finish the pies for Thanksgiving." She took a step closer and threw her arms around him. "Welcome home, Lucas."

Lucy started toward her as if to say something, but Alex wiggled her fingers in a wave as she disappeared, almost as quickly as she'd arrived.

Hmhmmmmh.

Lucy cleared her throat, her fingers lingering against the soft-looking skin of her neck. When she turned back toward him, she smiled nervously as she walked to the opposite end of the couch and sat down, motioning for him to do the same.

He sat.

"Mr. Deardon, I hope your reasons for coming to Whisper Ridge are admirable. I know he sent for you, but Liam is a very generous man and I would hate to see anyone take advantage of him. No one seems to know much, if anything, about you."

Sent for me? He leaned a little closer to her.

"Honestly, I expected to meet a child when you arrived, not...not..." she met his eyes, a dark pink staining her cheeks. "Well, you're not a child."

"No." He chuckled quietly and smiled, hoping to put her more at ease.

She returned his smile.

"Sorry," she said, raising her hands in the air and dropping them again in her lap. "I guess I'm a little nervous."

Honest. He liked that.

"It's no surprise that no one here knows much about me or my family, ma'am. I haven't been here at Whisper Ridge since I was five years old." Lucas did not feel like recounting how his father had been disinherited and had kept all of his children away from their grandfather for so long. Besides, she probably already knew enough about them to know that, and he'd rather not know exactly how much she knew.

Sent for him? The idea needled him again.

Silence passed between them for only a moment before he couldn't hold his tongue any longer. "I'm sorry, did you say he *sent* for me?" He just couldn't get the notion out of his head.

"Yes, of course. That *is* what the letter said, isn't it?" Her hand flew to the curve of her neck, her fingers caressing the indent there. "I'm afraid I just assumed..." She met his eyes. "Isn't that why you are here?"

"I haven't heard from my grandfather in as long as I've been gone from this place, ma'am. There wasn't any letter." Then, he remembered the post Noah had found in their father's office just before they'd left. The one he'd said was someone trying to stir up some trouble, and he wondered if it had indeed been written by their granddad.

A look of astonishment touched her eyes and froze her smile.

"No worries, ma'am." He moved to stand. "I'll just come back at a more convenient time, when he's home."

"Excuse me," she said softly as she stood up, her hand across her chest. "Whether he sent for you or not, I just know Liam would want to see you again. How long are you in town?"

"That depends on how long before I'm able to speak with him and tell him what I've come to say."

"Are you staying in Thistleberry?"

He shook his head. "Just arrived. Came here first thing."

"Well, let me see if I can't get Denver to make you up a bed in the bunkhouse. Alex said we should keep you a surprise, but I think Hank and Sam would like to know you're here. I'm sure they'll want to see you as much as Liam." She excused herself from the room before he could stop her.

Lucas had been so focused on making amends with his grandfather that the idea of reacquainting with the rest of them had his stomach in knots.

What will I say? How will they react?

He glanced around, stepping out into the entry and taking in the massive space. The hallway led into a great room with ceilings that extended to what he guessed was three or four times his own six feet and some. A picture on the top of the piano caught his attention. He strode over to the instrument and picked up the ornate silver frame with a photograph he immediately recognized as his brothers and him when he was only two–maybe three at most.

Can't be that angry still if he keeps our photograph out where he can see it.

"Do you play?" the woman asked when she returned.

He set the picture back on the piano and took a step away. "The piano? Um, no. Not much of a fan."

Her eyes widened in apparent surprise. "How can you be Liam's kin and not like music?"

Lucas shrugged. "I used to. A long time ago."

An older gentleman with a wide brimmed hat and a thick mustache stepped into the room, his hands folded over one another in front of him.

Lucy stared at him a moment longer, then turned to nod at the man. "Mr. Deardon, this is Denver. Your horse has already been seen to in the stables. You can collect your things there and then he'll show you where you'll be sleeping for the night."

Lucas turned to follow Denver, who he guessed to be the foreman, but stopped just short of her.

"Thank you, Miss...Lucy was it?"

"Yes," she replied with a quick smile. "Lucy Russell."

"Well, Miss Russell," he offered, looking at her, "I'm a might obliged. Thank you," he said, returning his hat to his head. "This certainly wasn't the way I'd expected to be greeted."

"I hope to be seeing more of you, Mr. Deardon. I'll let you know as soon as your grandfather returns." Her smile warmed him. She was beautiful.

"Ma'am," he tapped the brim of his Stetson with a nod and then stepped in line behind Denver and followed him out to collect his things from the stable.

CHAPTER FOUR

The snow fell more heavily now. While the weather had been quite cold, and at times near freezing over the last few weeks on the trail, he'd made good time and had thankfully arrived at Whisper Ridge without losing any of his fingers or toes.

"I'm guessing you're no stranger to ranch work," the man said, eyeing Lucas closely as he opened the front door to the bunkhouse. Several beds lined each wall and a hefty, circular table had been placed in the center of the large room.

"No, sir. Been working with horses my whole life." He stepped inside. "My family owns a ranch back in Oregon. We all have our jobs to do."

"I know'd your granddad owned lots of property. Doesn't surprise me none that y'all have a place out there." Denver sniffed at the air. "Well, we're grateful for the extra set of hands. Especially on a day like today." He glanced out the still open door then back at him as he stepped outside. "You sure look like a Deardon, now let's see if you work like one." He nodded at a bed with linens and blankets folded neatly at the foot. "You can bunk there for the night. Get yourself settled, then meet me out in the stables in a quarter hour." He tipped his hat and disappeared.

After Lucas set his things down next to the bed, he unfolded the covers and quickly pulled them tightly over the mattress, grateful he would not have to spend another night on the cold, hard ground.

As requested, he met Denver out at the stables and spent the next hour securing shutters, hauling wood into the homestead and bunkhouse, and feeding the horses in the biggest stable Lucas had ever seen. The stalls had already been mucked and the horses groomed, he just needed to make sure they had plenty of food and water until their next feeding.

There was something cathartic about working on his grandfather's ranch. Some of the dread that he'd experienced garnering the courage to knock on that front door seemed to dissipate with each new task he accomplished.

"Lucas."

He pricked his ears, unsure whether or not he'd heard the faint sound of his name carried on the breeze. When he didn't hear it again, he returned to his work, tossing the last barrow full of hay into the stall.

"Lucas!"

It was louder this time, clear as day. Someone *had* called his name. He scraped the pitchfork clean of debris, set it in the wheelbarrow, and headed for the front of the stables with an empty feed bucket and a tool crate.

As he rounded the edge of the long string of stalls, an older, gruff looking man, his stature nearly filling the door, stepped into the stable, clutching onto the top boards of the first stall.

"Lucas!" A crack broke in the man's voice as he called out his name again. "You made it."

Lucas set down his cargo and stared at him, eyes narrowed, hoping for some sense of recognition.

Granddad? He didn't trust himself to speak the name aloud.

"Lucas, is that really you?" the older man's whispered voice broke with emotion and he rushed forward, throwing his arms around his grandson and squeezing hard before pushing him away far enough to see his face. "Let me look at ya."

"Hello, Granddad. I'm Lucas." He'd prepared what he was going to say over and over again during his weeks on the trail, but at this moment, his mind was nothing more than a blank slate. He didn't trust himself to say anything else at that moment, for fear his voice would crack too.

"Of course you are. And you're a right grown man."

Lucas cleared his throat. "Yes, sir."

Granddad draped his arm around him and walked with him to the edge of the barn. "Lucy said you've holed up in the bunkhouse. But, I've got her seeing to it now that you have a nice room of your own inside the main house." He turned away and coughed into his shoulder, then squeezed Lucas's arm.

Arggg! Sharp pains shot up his shoulder and into his back. He bit his lip and tensed his hands. *Breathe, Deardon!* He would stand here for an eternity, pain and all, if it meant having his grandfather welcome him with open arms.

"My grandson. Here. And in time for the holiday feast." He coughed again. "I never would have believed it. It's been so long." Granddad clasped Lucas hard on the shoulder again, then released him.

Lucas grunted inwardly, flexing his jaw against the pain. Relief mixed with regret as the ache from his grandfather's grip subsided as did the welcoming feeling of his touch. The man's tenderness surprised him.

"Supper is almost ready. We've got a lot to catch up on. Go get your things and meet me inside."

"Yes, sir. Right after I put blankets on all of the remaining horses."

Granddad stood still for a moment, just staring at him. His

chest puffed out slightly and he smiled crookedly. Then, he nodded and ducked out into the increasingly cold storm toward the house, lifting his arms to protect him from the onslaught of snow that now fell in droves.

Cough. Cough. The cough could be heard above the rush of strong winds.

That doesn't sound good.

Lucas scrunched his brows together. The man he'd just met, his grandfather, was not a man who never wanted to see his grandchildren again.

"Dad lied," he whispered to himself. To hear his father tell it, Liam Deardon was a hard man—impossible even with nary an ounce of compassion. How many times had he heard over the years that their grandfather was too stubborn to allow them to visit? How many times had they needlessly felt rejected by people they loved?

Too many.

He'd lied. What other explanation could there be?

The only empty bedroom in the house that still had a bed was the one right across from Lucy's.

"What are you doing to me, Liam?" she asked aloud, though under her breath.

The idea of such a beautiful man's quarters so close to hers both thrilled and alarmed her. What of propriety? She'd already been distracted from her duties all day just thinking about Liam's grandson and was worried that nothing would ever get done with him around. And with all the festivities later in the week, there was still plenty to do, despite the imposing weather.

The back door opened and closed. Instinctively, Lucy checked her reflection in the dark window's glass and immediately chastised herself for her vanity. Heavy footfalls against the wooden floor set the pit of her stomach into chaos. Her plans for the day had been disrupted by the storm and she wasn't sure what to do with herself, so she quickly escaped into the kitchen to help with supper, only to find Liam seated at the head of the table.

He looked up. "Ah, Lucas, my boy. Sit. Sit."

Lucy's brows furrowed and she turned back to look over her shoulder.

"Excuse me," a deep, resonant voice cooed in low tones from behind her. He cradled her elbow as he guided her out of his path, making his way into the kitchen and to the Deardon-sized dinner table. A tingling sensation rippled up her arms and over the whole of her at his brazen touch.

That will be enough of that. You don't know anything about this man.

Of course she hadn't known anything about Gilroy Hearn either and she had committed to marry him through a mere exchange of several letters over a relatively short period of time. Look where that had gotten her. She stopped herself before mustering any ill will. After all, something good had come of the situation. She should thank Mr. Hearn for running off with the shop-keep's daughter. She would have never met Liam Deardon or his family had it not been for the cheat.

Her thoughts were interrupted when Liam coughed. His breathing had a slight wheeze to it and the overall tone to his skin was pallid, even though his cheeks were flushed. She didn't know why she hadn't seen it before. She guessed she had just been too excited to see him after weeks of being away. But the robust man she'd come to know and love, looked overly tired and she made a mental note to have a nice, hot bath drawn and a fire stoked in his hearth. The man obviously needed some rest after his journey.

Cough.

"Liam," she asked as she approached the table, "how long have you had that cough?"

"Ah, don't concern yourself with me, Lucy Mae. It's nothing." He waved to her. "Come. Sit with us. I was just going to talk to Lucas about my letters."

Lucy's feet would not move toward them. Couldn't. She smiled apologetically. "I think we'll just wire the doctor first. I know he's in Thistleberry today, but he has a new apprentice," she hoped that's what he was called, "who I am sure can finish his rounds in town. I'll be right back." She took a step toward Liam's office.

"If you're already headed all the way into town, why would you need to wire him?" Lucas asked, his confusion understandable.

Lucy wasn't quite sure how to respond.

"I'm just heading into your grandfather's study."

"Are you telling me that you have a telegraph here? In the house?" Lucas asked, awe and incredulity apparent in his voice.

She ignored him and took another step.

"Look outside, Lucy." Liam motioned toward the window. "I'm not going to risk him coming out in this weather for a simple little cough. There is nothing he can do right now that a cup of hot tea won't cure."

"I'll just put a pot on the stove, then."

"Sit!" he said firmly. "Please." His voice softened. "I want you to get to know your betrothed."

"Her what?" Lucas demanded, echoing her surprise. He pushed back the chair and was on his feet in an instant. He looked at Lucy, then back at Liam. "Whoa. Wait a minute. I never agreed to get married. Not to anyone."

"Liam," Lucy looked up at him with a smile she hoped would convince him to listen to her, "I thought we'd agreed. No more matchmaking." She should be surprised at what her benefactor had clearly written in his letters, but she wasn't. He had felt responsible for her situation from the beginning and had made it his mission to find her the right husband.

Lucas had told her that he hadn't received any of his

grandfather's letters, but still, the disappointment at his obvious aversion to even the idea of marrying her stung.

"That's why you're here, isn't it? You got my letters and you came to fulfill an old man's wish?"

"Sorry, Granddad. Miss Lucy said you sent us a letter right after she got here, but if that's so, we never received it. At least not that I know of. And I sure as h—" he swallowed the last word and looked over at her. "I didn't see it," he amended.

Liam glanced between her and his grandson, then he motioned for her to join them at the table.

She stayed put for as long as she dared, but Liam Deardon had been good to her and she didn't have the heart to deny him. She complied with his wishes and took the seat across the table from Lucas. Liam reached out and squeezed her hand with a wink, then turned his focus back to his grandson.

"Then, what is it that brought you to Whisper Ridge if it wasn't for my letters? For I thought surely Fate was smiling on me today." He winked.

Lucas cleared his throat and glanced at Lucy whose heart fluttered airily in her chest. She had to force herself to breathe.

Didn't you hear him, Lucy Russell? He's not looking to get married. To anyone.

After a moment's hesitation, Lucas reclaimed his seat at the table, keeping his head low, and staring at some invisible spot on the wood. His fingers fidgeted and he bit at his lip. It wasn't long before he finally spoke. "The Pony Express was our biggest contract buyer and with the telegraph now extending from one side of the country to the other, there's not much of a need for our horses. They are closing up shop." He scratched at the invisible spot.

Liam sat quietly and listened, waiting for him to continue.

"An opportunity came up," Lucas told them, "that will help us to save our ranch, but it requires a change in livestock. We won't be breeding and selling horses anymore, but cattle. We've always been horse ranchers and don't know anything about raising cattle, but Noah has hired on at our neighbors ranch to learn as much as he can."

Liam leaned back in his chair, still listening intently.

Lucas was quiet.

"Out with it, son. I sense a question in there somewhere. What is it?"

DING! CLANG! DING! CLANG! DING!

The hollow clang of the dinner triangle rang loudly and for longer than normal, but it wasn't suppertime. The kitchen door burst open and Denver stuck his head inside.

"We've got a problem."

CHAPTER FIVE

"Stampede in the pasture just beyond the gate!" Denver sucked in a breath and swallowed hard, slapping his gloves against his thigh. "Water tower's coming down if we don't hurry."

Liam, Lucas, and Lucy all shot to their feet at once.

"The mustang got out and scared the cows. Several of the men are trying to round them up now. Haven't seen the stallion."

"Anyone told Hank and Sam?"

Denver shook his head. "Not unless they heard the triangle ring."

"What can I do?" Lucas asked his grandfather, grabbing his hat from the back of the chair.

"You'll ride with me," Granddad directed him. "Lucy, honey, I need you to get Tillie and help her put a large pot of vittles over a fire. We're all going to be cold when we return and the men will need something to warm their bellies.

She nodded and with a worried glance at Lucas left the kitchen straightaway.

"Let's go," Liam said as he placed a hand behind Lucas's

back and pulled the door shut behind him.

It didn't take long to get the horses saddled and the wagon prepared, though the water tower was not that far off from the homestead. Lucas wondered at first why they didn't just head out there on foot, but when he saw the wealth of tools, lumber, and rope that had been loaded into the back he understood and climbed up into the driver's seat.

When they reached the water tower, Lucas looked up, squinting against the snow, surprised. He wasn't sure what he'd expected, but the enormous house-sized barrel sitting atop a raised wooden foundation held together by several leather-strapped poles and a few nails wasn't it. He'd seen similar contraptions at the Whittaker's place back home by the waterwheels in the lumberyards and once or twice at the edge of some of the bigger towns along the trail, but this was a first time seeing one on a single ranch. He wondered how it didn't freeze in the wintertime.

"If that tower comes down," his grandfather told him as they unloaded the supplies, "it'll flood that stable." He nodded at a small building that looked like it could hold ten, maybe fifteen, mounts. "There will be no place for the new arrivals."

Whistles and hollers from the men, whips cracking the chilled air, and the restless, bellowing cattle mixed together for a cacophony of chaos. The setting sun, barely visible through the billowy snowflakes scattering across the ground, gave just enough light for the small crew to start shoring up a number of the fractured braces.

Lucas tossed his hat under the foot rest of the buckboard, strapped one of the large poles over his good shoulder, and after bypassing a few of the injured cattle, headed up the ladder. Once the post was in place, chocked up against one of the broken ones, Denver worked to secure a length of rope around and through both pieces.

CRACK!

One of the cows lying at the base of the tower dropped

lifeless in a heap and Lucas looked up to see his grandfather, rifle in hand, move to where the next one cried up at him.

CRACK!

Lucas closed his eyes. He hated to lose livestock to the unexpected.

The tower wavered, the earsplitting sound of wood splintering apart shoving Lucas's stomach into his throat.

"Look out," Denver yelled as the last cow rolled into the remaining brace and knocked it free.

As the tower leaned toward his granddad, Lucas and the foreman both jumped free of the contraption, and with a deafening crash, the water rushed from the shattered pieces of the container.

Lucas groaned as he hit the ground, but he wasn't hurt. Immediately, he jumped to his feet, looking for any sign of his grandfather.

"Granddad," he yelled to be heard over the added ruckus of flowing water and scanned the area, sloshing back and forth, searching in the icy-cold, knee-deep rivulet wreaking havoc on the landscape for any sign of the man. "Granddad," he yelled again.

Cough. Cough. Cough.

Lucas whipped his head toward the stable. There in the shallows of the flooding snow-covered grasses his grandfather gripped a hold of one of the knots in a log and dragged himself up out of the water, sputtering and shivering. Lucas lifted his legs and ran as fast as he could through the high drainage and draped the man's arms over his shoulders and dragged him to dry earth.

He lay down on the ground next to his grandfather, his hand resting over the violent pounding of his heart and he gasped for air. After a moment, he turned on his side to look at Liam.

"Damn that water's cold," Granddad said with a forced chuckle.

Lucas fell back against the fresh layers of snow and snorted a laugh.

"Mr. Deardon, are you all right?" Denver stood over his grandfather, helping the man into a seated position and handed him his sopping hat.

"A few hours next to the hearth and we'll both be right as rain," Granddad said.

Lucas pulled himself to his feet. Luckily, the tower had fallen away from the wagon and they would not have to walk even the short distance back. He helped Liam up onto the buckboard's bench and made quick work of unsaddling his grandfather's horse. After handing the reins to Denver, and tossing the saddle into the back next to the cow some of the men had loaded, he climbed up next to Liam and wrapped the saddle blanket around the man's shivering shoulders and started back to the homestead as quickly as he dared in this weather and light.

"So," Liam broke their silence, "I believe you had a question to ask me."

Lucas looked over at the man, grateful he couldn't distinguish his features completely.

"Well?"

"It can wait, Granddad."

"Maybe, but I want to hear it now. Out with it."

Lucas looked down at the reins in his hands. "Well, sir," he cleared his throat, "when we were out at Redbourne Ranch last year visiting Aunt Leah, Raine mentioned something about…well, about there being a special inheritance we could receive on our wedding day if we marry before the age of twenty-five."

"That's right. Can't have you boys becoming too incorrigible now, can I? I figure I might as well be able to watch you all enjoy it some before I'm gone. Though, you'd be the first."

Lucas looked up and with a firm set to his jaw, he met

Liam's eyes. "Not me. Nooooo," he shook his head again. "But, I am here. Asking. I know you didn't want to see us anymore and we've been disinherited and all…"

Liam opened his mouth to say something, but Lucas didn't give him the chance. He'd practiced this speech a thousand times over and had to get it all out.

"But I was wondering if you might reconsider. Just this once." He held up his hand before Liam could answer. "If not, I understand and simply ask that I might have a job at Whisper Ridge with a fair wage. I work real hard and I'm willing to do just about anything. But, first…" he took off his hat and ran his fingers through his too-long hair. "First, I want to know why you did that. Why? Why did you ban us from Whisper Ridge? Why did you disinherit us? Didn't you care about us anymore?" Lucas locked eyes again with his grandfather, then returned to their path.

CHAPTER SIX

"Disinherit you?" Cough. "Why, I didn't disinherit you, Lucas. How could I? You're my kin. My flesh and blood. You didn't do anything wrong. No matter what your pa's told you, I love you, son. You and your brothers." He paused. "And your pa. Always have."

Lucas fought the emotion that sprung to his eyes. He swallowed the lump that formed in his throat and focused on getting them back through the deepening snow.

When he pulled into the barn, the stable hand and a few of the men stood waiting to tend to the wagon. Lucas helped his grandfather to the ground.

"I'm fine, son. Just craving some of Tillie's vittles about now." He pushed his way through the door, cursing when he stumbled slightly over the threshold.

Warmth from the stone hearth welcomed them inside with its comforting embrace. Lucas shivered lightly as he tried to shake off the cold.

"Liam," Lucy exclaimed as she rushed to the man's side, "what's happened? Are you all right? Is anyone hurt?"

He didn't stop to answer, but kept walking toward the staircase. "We're soaked to the bone, Lucy Mae." He rubbed his hands together. "Will you pour us a bowl of those steaming vittles and set on a pot of tea?" he asked as he climbed onto the first step.

She nodded.

"That's my girl," he said with a wink and scrambled up the rest of the stairs.

"We were lucky," Lucas said as he stepped toward the staircase. "No one got hurt."

"Thank you," she mouthed with a relieved smile before turning back for the kitchen.

When he reached the top of the stairs, his grandfather had already disappeared behind closed doors at the end of the hall. He ducked inside his room. While there was a small hearth in the corner, no fire had been set ablaze. The air still held a chill, but for now, he'd settle for dry clothes. He laid his coat over the arm of the chair and set his soaked boots next to the door. At least he'd brought one extra pair. His Sunday best.

He shrugged into a fresh pair of long johns and clean denim trousers.

SLAM!

Lucas nearly jumped out of his skin. The shutters on his bedroom window had burst open and shut. It was a wonder they hadn't broken the glass. He guessed the second level windows had not yet been secured. He shook his head, slipped on a dry pair of socks and tugged on his Sunday boots.

Knock. Knock.

"What's taking you so long?" his grandfather asked from the other side of the door.

Lucas swung it open to the teasing smile on the man's face.

"Come on. It's a lot warmer down by the fire." Granddad stopped midway down the steps, turned his head, nose scrunched. "Achoo!" He nodded curtly and finished his descent.

As they walked into the kitchen, two large bowls of steaming liquid accompanied by a small basket of hot and flaky butter biscuits welcomed them at the table. Lucas sat down and wrapped his stiff hands around the warm bowl. He looked up when Lucy started to giggle. His grandfather also had his hands clasped around his dish.

"They say it's like father like son, but I think the old adage applies," she said with a smile. "Here. I thought you both might want something special. Tillie picked some up while she was in town."

Lucas set his bowl down and took the mug from her. He looked down into the hot brown liquid swirled with fresh cream.

"What is it?"

"Hot chocolate." Lucy's tongue ran over her lips and she closed her eyes with an innocent shrug. "I haven't had any since I left New York. Isn't it wonderful?"

Lucas shifted in his chair and chuckled. He'd only had hot chocolate once before that he could remember. At Redbourne Ranch. He smiled at the memory and brought the warm cup up to his lips, careful not to drink it too quickly. He'd made that mistake before and nearly burnt the buds from his tongue.

The distinct taste of peppermint caressed his mouth with fresh, creamy indulgence. The sweet treat trailed warmth down his throat to his belly and he shivered as the cold was forced outward.

"Thank you, Miss Russell."

Lucy pulled a blanket from a large basket at the foot of the fireplace and tossed it over Granddad's shoulders. From what Lucas could gather, Lucy hadn't been at Whisper Ridge very long, but she fit here. He couldn't explain how he knew. He just did. It was easy to see how much she'd already grown to care for his grandfather and the others on the ranch.

"I don't know how I ever survived without her here," Granddad said as they both watched her retreat behind the counter to help the cook with vittles for the rest of the men.

Silence passed between them for a few minutes while they slurped their warm food.

"I miss you boys, more than most anything in the world, I reckon. Apart from your Grandma Sophia, God rest her soul," he spoke into his soup. "That's why I wanted to invite you all here to Whisper Ridge for the holidays." He turned to look at Lucas. "I want you all to be a part of the family you came from. To learn about and understand your heritage. Who you are. Being a Deardon is a noble thing. I don't want you to be away from me, son. I want you to be here. *With* me. With all of us."

Cough.

"You...what?" Lucas pushed his empty bowl away from him and turned to look at his grandfather. "All this time. And I thought...I thought you..." he shook his head back and forth, unsure of what to say. "You really *do* want to see us, don't you? To be a part of our lives?"

Granddad nodded his affirmation. "You're here now, aren't ya? And I'm offering you the chance to claim the inheritance that young Raine can only speculate on." He looked over at Lucy and nodded in her direction. "That *is* what you want, right?" There was a twinkle in his eyes, despite his now sunken features.

"Not exactly. Well, yes, but," Lucas paused, "it's not for me." Lucas smiled awkwardly. "See it's—"

"Of course, not. It's for your ranch. Your father and brothers." Granddad scratched his jawline with the back of his fingers.

"Yes, but I'm not the one—"

"Mmmmhmmmm," Granddad said, disbelievingly as he raised a brow, his lips protruding slightly, as he bobbed his head. "We'll just let that sit for a bit. Now, tell me everything. I want to hear about you and your brothers." He pushed his chair away from the table and leaned back, arms folded. "How is that stubborn son of mine?" He fired out one question right after another.

Lucas stared at his granddad a long while before answering. How could he fill the man in on everything in their lives in just one conversation?

I can't, he relented. *But, God willing, we'll have a lifetime to catch up.*

So much had happened. Where did he begin?

"Mama ran off a long time ago."

"I'd heard that." Granddad undid the top button on his shirt and pulled the collar away from his neck. "I always did think she was too big for her britches. Sorry, son. I know that must have been hard on you boys."

"It's simple really and, like I said before, it was a long time ago." He shrugged. "She was given an opportunity and she took it. Singing on a stage in Chicago. She never looked back."

"And you haven't heard from or seen her since?"

"Nope. Not interested. She made her choice and we've learned to live with it." He picked up his mug and sipped down the last of his hot chocolate. The cup tinged against the wood when he set it back down on the table. "And then Henry..." Lucas paused, checking the emotion in his voice. "Henry died, Granddad. Last year."

His grandfather's expression turned solemn and his jaw flexed with emotion. He swallowed hard. "Your Aunt Leah told me it was an accident." He turned back to the table and rested his elbows on its top. "Those wild mustangs, for all their beauty and spirit, can be downright devilish. I ought to know." He turned to look at Lucas and raised a brow. "Been thrown from enough of 'em."

"You break mustangs?" Lucas wasn't sure why that surprised him, but it gave him a higher appreciation for the aging man. "I didn't remember that about you, Granddad. Honestly, I don't remember much about any of this." Lucas pointed out the window with a nudge of his chin.

"I don't ride much anymore. I'm getting on in years, but

don't let anyone know I've admitted that. I leave the wild ones to Hank, Sam, and their boys. A man could get himself killed if he's not careful." His eyes widened immediately as if realizing the mistake in his words. "Forgive an old man his thoughtlessness, son."

Lucas stole a glance at Lucy. She was busy ladling stew into bowls, careful to avoid his gaze.

"He didn't suffer," he said with the shake of his head, "but it hit us all pretty hard."

Silence passed between them again for a short time.

"Well, he's with the good Lord now." He patted Lucas on the hand. "I've got a confession to make, son."

Cough.

Lucy raised her head to look at them, her eyebrows scrunched together and her ear turned slightly toward them.

Granddad leaned forward, his elbows on his knees, and dropped his head.

Lucas sat up straight and narrowed his eyes.

"I know about Markham and the offer he's made your father."

Lucas wasn't sure what he had expected the man to say, but that was not it. He furrowed his brow. "How could you possibly know about that?"

"You don't get to be where I'm at without learning a few tricks," he said, raising his head to look at Lucas. "After my Leah sent word about Henry, I wrote to a friend of mine in Oregon, who filled me in on your predicament. Of course, I knew that your father would never accept my help, so I made a purchase on his behalf. With his money. It was an offer Mr. Markham could not refuse."

Granddad pushed off his knees and leaned back against the chair. His face was flushed. His eyes glassy.

Lucy quickly pumped a glass of water and rushed toward them. "Liam, you look like you are feeling ill. Is everything all right?" It was as if she could sense that something was wrong.

She set the drink on the table in front of his grandfather—
concern evident on her brow.

"Just a little warm now is all. Thank you, Lucy Mae." He
lifted the glass to her and took a large gulp. "Maybe we should
go for a little walk."

Lucy shot a look at Lucas that betrayed her worry. A
storm raged outside. They would not be going for a walk.

"The paperwork for the herd is being drawn up as we
speak. It now belongs to your family. It was paid for out of a
portion of your father's estate. The money he left behind."
Granddad laughed, then coughed. "You said before that Noah
has hired on with Markham. Well, when he heads for home,
he'll do so with a full herd and the drovers to help him get
them there."

Lucas didn't know what to say—something that had never
been much of a problem at home, much to Jonah's chagrin.
But here, it seemed almost commonplace.

"It's done? The herd's been paid for?"

Granddad nodded.

"I know you've already got a full crew, but I'm a real hard
worker and have been working the horse ranch near my whole
life."

"What are you talking about, Lucas?"

"I can work off our debt."

"Haven't you been listening to a word I've said? It wasn't
my money to pay back. It rightfully belongs to your father. I
just helped him spend it." Granddad guffawed, which quickly
turned to a bellowing cough.

Lucas frowned as he patted his grandfather on the back.
"I listened. It's just more than I possibly could have expected."

Liam tsked. "It must have been hard on you boys.
Growing up without a mother."

Lucas nodded. "Or a grandfather."

"Ha," Granddad chuckled. "You're straightforward, kid. I
like that." Cough. "Now, let me be straight with you." He

reached out and took Lucy by the hand and pulled her close to him as he spoke to Lucas. "I want you to stay at Whisper Ridge. I've missed out on too many years to lose you again. I want to know my grandsons. I understand you not wanting to get married, what with your mama the way she is and all, but Lucy needs a good man. A Deardon man."

Why didn't I bring Noah?

CHAPTER SEVEN

"Liam, please." Lucy's heart pounded heavily in her chest. It was one thing to agree to marry a stranger after exchanging dozens of letters through the mail, but quite another to be pawned off on a reluctant groom. "I told you. I want to do it right this time. I want to fall in love."

"You want a husband, don't you, girl? Babies?"

Heat flooded Lucy's face. She couldn't look at Lucas for fear of the rejection she would see there. "Of course, but not like this." She knew Liam felt responsible for her, but he'd already given her a home and had seen to it that she'd learned what she needed to survive a life in the west. That was enough.

"Let's get one thing straight in all of this," Lucas looked between them, "I am *not* ready to get married. To anyone." He met her gaze fully with a raised brow. "No matter how pretty…or perfect she might be."

Lucy's cheeks burned. She did not want to be the first one to look away, but heaven help her, if she kept staring at him, she might forget her place.

Why does he have to be so handsome?

Cough. Cough. Liam's cough was getting worse by the

minute.

Lucy broke contact to look at the man who'd become like a father to her.

Something's wrong.

His heavily lidded eyes shone like glass.

"Your father left," Liam said simply. "I thought I...I would give him some time to blow off steam, but...but he never came back. I didn't believe he would deprive his children of their grandfather." His face grew increasingly red and his skin had developed a tight sheen. "I was...wrong," he whispered.

"Liam?"

Knock. Knock.

The back door opened and a dozen ranch hands came in, collected a bowl of vittles, and with nary a tip of their hats, retreated to the bunkhouse to eat their hot meal. She wondered why it had taken them so long to come in after they'd returned, but guessed after being out in the weather, they'd all had to change.

She looked back at Liam. "What exactly happened out there?" she demanded.

"It's nothing, Lucy. I'm just more tired than I thought. Don't you worry none." He grabbed the glass she'd brought over earlier and guzzled the rest of it down as if it contained something a little more spirited.

She shot a questioning glance at Lucas.

"We lost the water tower. He didn't get hurt, but he was caught up in the runoff and drenched in the icy water."

"I'm fine. I think I'll just go sit in my favorite chair and read for a spell." Liam pushed himself out of his wooden seat and pulled one of the already lit lanterns from the collection of lights overhead and started for the living area.

He only got a few steps before he collapsed onto the floor. The lantern shattered and one of the small floor rugs caught fire. Lucas picked up the woven carpet and beat the edges together until the flames had been extinguished.

"Liam!" Lucy screamed as she rushed to him, knelt down at his side, and shook his shoulders as well as she could from her position. She lifted his head and patted his face. "Liam. Wake up."

Cough. Cough. Cough.

She put a hand against Liam's forehead. "He's burning up."

He moaned, but didn't appear able to lift his head on his own.

Lucas picked Lucy up by the shoulders and set her aside, then crouched down, gathered his grandfather into his arms, and headed for the door.

"What are you doing?" Her breathing grew ragged, her heart raced. "What are you doing?" she demanded again as she followed him out into the near blizzard of a storm.

Lucas pushed through the gate at the front of the house where grass normally grew. He laid Liam on the ground and began to scoop snow on top of him. He covered his arms, his neck, his head, everywhere but his face.

"Stop it!" she screamed as she pulled hard at his arm and shoulder.

"Ahhhhh!" Lucas cried out in pain, startling her enough that she took a step back from him.

"Please stop," she pleaded. What else could she say?

Please, God, make him stop.

"Go back in the house!" Lucas demanded loud enough to be heard above the deafening wind, but he continued to cover his grandfather until he was completely buried in the cold, packed snow.

Once Lucas stood up and backed away from Liam, she rushed toward him, but Lucas grabbed her and pulled her into his embrace. She pounded against him and writhed as if her life, or Liam's, depended on it.

"Shhhhh," he whispered against her hair, causing a stream of melting snow to trail the back of her head and down her neck.

She shivered.

"We have to break the fever. This is the fastest way I know." His lips touched the top of her head with a comforting kiss.

His words made sense, but it took a moment before she could allow herself to relax against this stranger who had come into their lives in a whirlwind. It pained her to see Liam this way.

"Let's get you inside by the warmth of the hearth fire and I will sit with him for as long as it takes. You'll need to keep the fire stoked," he instructed, "and be ready with warm blankets and dry clothes. When his fever finally submits, he'll sweat it out and in order to keep him from catching a chill, we'll need to dry him quickly and keep him warm."

She didn't want to move, couldn't stand the thought of leaving Liam on the ground in the snow, even for a moment. Lucas finally let go of her, but she stayed, despite the growing chill that triggered an involuntary shudder to cascade from her shoulders downward.

"Either you go of your own volition or I'll carry you back in the house over my shoulder." Lucas's warning was firm, but not unkind. His face, determined.

I believe he would.

She stood her ground a moment longer, but when he started toward her, she held up her hands and turned for the house.

Although Lucas was a Deardon, he was still a perfect stranger. She glanced back at him.

Can I trust him?

All she had left was hope.

Yes, she determined, *I believe I can.* But that didn't mean she couldn't wire for the good doctor. She picked up her skirt and headed inside.

CHAPTER EIGHT

Lucas rubbed his bare hands together and brought them up to his mouth, his breath providing momentary warmth against the chilly winter's eve. He looked down at the man lying still in the mound of snow at his feet, wanting desperately to take away his pain. He hadn't left his granddad's side for the better part of half an hour, watching, waiting for any sign that the fever had broken. There was still so much to say. To hear. To repair.

Whoosh!

A fierce gust of wind racked the boarded windows on the barn and the shutters on the house shook. Beads of sweat finally appeared on Liam's forehead.

Lucas jumped up off the milking stool he had retrieved from the barn and without taking the time to brush the snow from his grandfather, he shoved his arms beneath the old man's ailing body and heaved him upward. When he reached the back door, it flung open wide.

Lucy had been watching from the window.

"In here," she instructed.

He followed her into the house, down the hallway, and up

the stairs to a spacious room with an enormous bed in the center and a hearth on one side, aglow with a roaring fire. She folded back the bedding, handed him a man's dry night shirt and a large towel. By their feel, she had taken great care to warm them by the fire. She turned around to face the stone fireplace.

Lucas gently laid his grandfather down on the bed, leaning him up against several pillows that had been recently fluffed. He hastily tugged the man's clothing from his cold, wet body and replaced them with the dry, striped night garment. Once Liam was tucked nicely between the sheets, Lucy handed Lucas a cream-colored linen bundle.

"I also heated some rocks in the fire. I thought they might help to keep the bedding warm."

Lucas lifted the blankets at the foot of the bed and inserted the toasty package.

"Thank you." Those two little words had been extremely hard to voice with his throat so swollen with emotion. He didn't trust himself to say more.

"Where is he?" the sound of a man's voice carried up from the bottom of the stairs.

Lucy rushed to the door. "We're in here, Doc."

It wasn't long before a short little man appeared in the doorway and removed his snow covered hat, tossing it into a large chair in the corner of the room, as he hurried to Liam's side. He placed the back of his hand against the sick man's forehead and breathed out a sigh that sounded much like relief.

"I thought you said he was burning up, Miss Lucy." The doctor pulled a metal stethoscope from his black bag, placing the buds into his ears and the flat, round side against his grandfather's chest. "He's scarcely a fever."

Lucas had seen a similar listening instrument when the vet had come to check on the horses back home at the ranch. He didn't need any tools to tell him how fast his own heart was beating.

"Mr. Deardon here," Lucy stepped toward the physician, pointing to Lucas, "packed him in a mound of snow out back to cool him down."

The doctor shot a look that measured the length of him. "Deardon, huh?" he asked as he returned his focus to the patient.

"Yes, sir. I'm his grandson. Lucas."

"Ah...Gabe's kid?"

"Yes, sir."

It still surprised Lucas how everyone seemed to remember his father, even though they'd been gone for many years. The folks around Thistleberry all seemed to have lived there a long time.

"Wasn't sure we'd see any of you back around these parts after everything that happened." The doc looked up over the end of his nose. "He here?"

And they all know everybody else's business.

"No, sir. We have a ranch over in Oregon territory. He and my brother, Jonah, are handling our affairs there."

"Oregon Territory?" The doc wrapped up his medical instrument and returned it to his bag. "That's a might cry from here, son."

"Yes, sir."

Liam coughed again, drawing the attention of everyone in the room.

"He takes after his granddad, don't ya think, Thomas?" Liam's voice was low and scratchy.

Lucas snapped his head toward the bed. His granddad's lips looked dry and cracked, but his eyes fluttered open and he blinked a few times before they stayed that way.

"Good lookin' boy, ain't he?"

The doctor laughed and shook his head. "You're as stubborn as they come, Deardon." The doc leaned over him, gently pulling at the skin below his eyes and looking them over. "Your grandson, Gabe's boy I hear," he reached up and patted him on the shoulder, "done real good burying you in that snow out there. Saved your life, if you ask me."

An odd sense of pride seemed to work its way to the surface and relief washed over Lucas. He hadn't known what else to do, but he'd seen the doctor back home pack ice around a child with a fever and had prayed it would work.

Thank you.

"If Liam's fever was still as bad as Lucy said it was," the doc said to Lucas, "he certainly wouldn't be awake right now, let alone talking, if you hadn't been so quick thinking."

Lucy raised a large pitcher and poured some water into a tin cup and set it down on the night table. She wiggled her way in front of Lucas and gingerly lay down across his granddad's chest.

"I thought you…I thought…"

"Shhhh," Liam said, stroking her hair.

Cough.

She stood up, retrieved the cup, and placed it up against his lips.

Cough.

It spilled a little, but she was persistent.

"He's going to need plenty of rest," the doctor told them. "I'll stay in my quarters down the hall for the night." He nodded curtly and turned to leave the room, but stopped when he reached the door. "Where's Hank?"

Lucy stood up.

"I," she started and then cleared her throat. "I'd imagine he's still at home. With the weather being what it was, I needed Denver to collect you." She looked at Lucas. "Neither one of us was willing to leave his side."

He nodded appreciatively at her.

There had been several hands in the bunkhouse that could have possibly ridden out to get his uncles, but with the storm the way it was, they hadn't wanted to chance another mishap and there was nothing Hank or Sam could have done, except worry. He tried to justify it in his mind, but the truth was, Lucas wasn't sure he was ready to meet them just yet. He'd just gotten his grandfather back. He couldn't lose him now.

"Smart girl," the doc told Lucy with a wink. He picked up his hat, the curve of a smile touching his face, and he walked out.

"The doctor has his own quarters in the house?" Lucas could hardly believe the extent of the wealth surrounding him at every turn. He thought of his own room back home that he shared with Noah. The oversized bunks took up the majority of the space, but they only needed it for sleeping. It had been plenty big. But staying here at Whisper Ridge, even for a short while, was going to take some getting used to. Not that he was complaining.

Lucy placed a hand on his forearm. "I'm sorry I doubted you."

CHAPTER NINE

Lucas nodded, then turned back to his grandfather and sat down on the edge of the bed, leaning over as if to be closer to the man.

"Jonah got married," he blurted. He wanted to tell his grandfather all the good things that had happened in their lives and not just the bad. He hadn't had that chance at dinner. "Emma is perfect for him. And dang pretty too. It's quite a story." He glanced over at Lucy who sat on the hearth with her elbows on her knees and her chin in her hands. He winked.

"Lucas?" his grandfather spoke with a low, scratchy voice as he reached up and touched his grandson's face. "I'm so glad you're really here."

Lucas closed his eyes with gratitude. With everything that had happened over the last few hours, he wasn't sure if his granddad would be able to recall their conversations. He reached up to take the old man's hand in his.

"Yes. I'm here."

Lucy stood up again and poured a glass of water, handed it to Lucas, and motioned at Liam with a nod of her head. Lucas gently placed one hand under his grandfather's head and placed the cup against his lips, willing him to drink. After only a couple of sips, he choked on the water and it drizzled down his chin.

"Argggg," Liam said disgustedly as he wiped it away with the back of his hand and pushed himself up into a seated position on the bed. "Now, there's no need to fuss over me." He took the cup from Lucas's hand. "I know you both feel like you have to hover, but I am a grown man and can drink for myself."

"Ha," Lucas laughed, evoking a reluctant smile from his grandfather.

"Of course you can, Granddad."

Liam set the glass on the night table.

"How are you feeling?" Lucy asked the older man from her position on the other side of the bed.

Granddad turned to look at her. "Like a herd of wild horses dragged me through an icy swamp." He shivered with exaggerated movements, but managed a smile. With an attempt to get out of the bed, he threw the covers off his legs and swung them over the edge.

"Oh, no you don't," Lucy said, jumping up and pushing gently against the old man's chest. "You have to rest. Doctor's orders." She threw the blankets back over him and brushed her hand across his forehead. "And you…" she said as she squinted her eyes at him, "are going to do what the doctor ordered."

Lucas couldn't help but admire the woman who'd demonstrated more than once over the last few hours her devotion to his grandfather. Who was she to him? And why was he so bent on making sure she became a part of the family?

"Come on, Luce. I'm feeling much better. Thanksgiving is near upon us and we've still got a lot to do to finish the preparations."

"Nonsense." She placed her hands on her hips. "Most everything has been in place for days. What's a little weather when a Deardon is involved? Besides, Lucas will help me with the final prep—"

"I will?"

She slapped him on the arm.

He cleared his throat. "I mean, I will!" he confirmed with conviction.

"Although," Lucy continued, "If this storm doesn't let up, we may have to postpone or even cancel the Thanksgiving tournament." A smile cracked on Lucy's face before her expression turned matter-of-fact.

Lucas smiled too.

"Cancel Thanksgiving?" Granddad bellowed, or at least he tried, but his cry lacked volume. "Why, Thanksgiving is a tradition around here. A rite of passage for my boys. Come hell or high water we're having the tournament."

"Oh, don't you go working yourself up into a tizzy," Lucy mock-scolded him. She glanced out the window. "It looks like the snow is letting up some. Denver and some of the others are still out there, so I think we'll just head out to check that everything will be ready. I'll stop by to see Hank on the way. He'll already be cross that I didn't tell him about this little episode sooner."

"My son will just blow everything out of proportion. You know that just as well as anyone. He'll be fine not knowing 'til morning." Granddad raised an eyebrow as if daring Lucy to go against his wishes.

She stared at the older man through squinted eyes, then a fully vibrant smile broke through. "The targets must be covered in a foot of snow by now. We'll have to get them brushed off before they freeze if you still want to have the archery and shooting competitions." She completely ignored his last comment. "Mara and Alex are bringing the pies tomorrow, Tillie has recruited several of the men to help with the food for the orphanage, and I'll speak with Denver about the big logs tomorrow."

Names swirled around in Lucas's head. Belonging to a big family was going to have its challenges and learning everyone's names and keeping them straight was going to be one of them.

"They are cabers, lassie. It is to be a caber toss to find the strongest of the lot."

Their grandmother had been born in Scotland, but it was odd hearing his granddad trying to imitate the brogue.

"Yes, yes, cabers," she waved at the air as if making a mental list of everything she needed to do. "Well, I think that just about does it."

"Luuucyyyy," Granddad said, a warning in his voice.

"Fine, I won't tell Hank. Until tomorrow," she clarified.

"What did I do all those years without you?" Liam asked through a tired smile.

Lucy smiled back.

"Goodnight, Mr. Deardon," she said with a playful shake to her head.

"Goodnight, Miss Russell. Or should I say soon-to-be Deardon?" He closed his eyes and lay back against the onslaught of pillows Lucy had stuck behind him. "Yep. Deardon. Now that it's settled, I think I might doze for just a wee bit," he made another attempt at his brogue. He coughed.

"You're incorrigible. We are not getting married, so stop pestering your grandson if you want him to stick around."

"Lucas. Son," Granddad opened his eyes and sat up straighter on the bed—with some effort, "I expect you'll be participating?"

"In what, exactly?" He liked Lucy, but he wasn't about to unwittingly agree to take on a Mrs. Lucas Deardon on a whim. Although the prospect didn't seem as terrifying as it had a few hours ago.

"In what?" Liam asked incredulously. "Didn't your father tell you any...?" his voice faded as he shook his head and mumbled something under his breath. He stopped and looked Lucas straight in the eye. "You're a Deardon..."

Lucas had the right name, but he sure felt like a foreigner with no idea what they would be doing to prepare for Thanksgiving. Back home, it was most like any other day, except, Dad paid Mrs. Markham to cook them up a fancy bird to eat with all the fixings. He imagined that Emma would be making something real special for those still at home. She was an excellent cook.

Cough.

Granddad sat up again. "…and you'll be competing in the Deardon's Thanksgiving Day Tournament, of course."

"We have a tournament?"

Lucy pushed Liam back against the fluffed pillows. "*If* the weather clears up," she amended. "Every year, the Deardons celebrate the holiday with a huge competition," she told Lucas. "There are three homesteads on Whisper Ridge. Liam's, Hank's, and Sam's. I guess your father never finished building his. Though you can see where he started."

Lucas had wondered what had ever happened to the foundation he'd seen his father working to build for their family—one of the only memories he still had of his time at Whisper Ridge.

"The others will start arriving first thing on Thursday morning." She patted Liam on the chest. "If *you* want to be well enough to get out of this bed and watch them, I suggest you get some rest."

"Yes, ma'am." Liam said, closing one eye, but keeping the other partially open, staring at her.

"What sort of competition?" Lucas rubbed his arm, which started to ache just thinking about what might await him. "And please tell me the teams are not divided into homesteads. I think ours would be slightly lacking." He managed a laugh.

"Come on," she pulled on his good arm.

He groaned, but followed her out of the room.

"It'll be grand," Granddad called after them.

"What sort of competition?" He repeated his question as

they descended the stairs.

When they reached the bottom, Lucy turned to him. "There's to be a log toss, an archery match, a stick pull, leg wrestling, and a riding course. I just hope we can pull it off with all this snow. It will certainly be a challenge."

There were no words. How was he supposed to hold his salt in a competition with his shoulder still causing him pain? Jonah told him before he left that he should give the injury time to mend, but he'd wanted to leave for Whisper Ridge as soon as he'd been able. The journey had proven more arduous than he had expected. Riding full days and sleeping on the cold, hard ground every night as he traveled to Montana hadn't helped the situation.

"You've had quite the long ride, Mr. Deardon, and with the water tower disaster and the unfortunate mishap with your grandfather, you must be exhausted. You don't have to participate if you're not feeling up to it. Your uncles and cousins won't think any less of you. And neither will I. Liam," she waved her hand up the stairs, "will get over it."

Lucas stared at her for a few moments.

Pain or not, Deardon, you are going to do this.

"Where do I sign up?" He pretended the crack in his voice had been on purpose.

Lucy giggled.

Lucas liked the sound.

CHAPTER TEN

"Good morning," Lucy crooned as she threw back the curtains in Liam's bedroom to allow in the brilliant beams of the morning's light. "Tillie made up some hot cakes, eggs, and bacon so you'll have a hearty breakfast to start off your day." She walked over to the table for the tray with the delicious collection of food.

With only one eye opened, Liam leaned up on one arm. "I'd forgotten how cheerful you can be when the sun comes up," he grumbled.

"You look like you are feeling much better," she said, happily.

"Yeah, thanks to that grandson of mine."

Lucy's face heated at the thought of the tall, handsome addition to Whisper Ridge.

"Where is that boy, anyway?"

"He's been up since the cock crowed near an hour ago." She placed the tray on his lap. "Helping Denver with the horses."

"So much fussin'. I can eat down at the table as well as anyone."

"Not today. Just let us spoil you for once."

"I need you to make good use of him this morning, Lucy. Show him around the place. I'd like him to stay on and don't want to waste any time getting him familiarized with the ranch. All of it."

"Well, I see my patient is up and talking." Doc pushed open the door a little farther and stepped into the room, his bag in hand. "How are you feeling this morning, Liam?"

"Right as rain. Ready to get back to work."

Doc looked from Liam to Lucy. "Under no circumstances is this man to leave this house today."

"Yes, sir," Lucy said with a smile. She knew it would be no easy feat, but it could be done. "You heard him," she said, pouring a glass of fresh milk, "doctor's orders."

Liam mumbled something under his breath just as he raised his cup to drink.

The spark was back in his eyes and that gave her comfort.

She turned to leave.

"Lucy Mae," Liam called.

She turned back to look at him.

"Lucas." He said his grandson's name as a reminder of what he'd asked of her.

She nodded. "I'll see to it that he's kept busy and out of trouble all day. And I'll be back to check in on you in a while." She skipped from the room and down the steps. After a very eventful day, she was ready for things to get back to normal— not that it was going to happen anytime soon. Especially with Lucas Deardon on the ranch. Whisper Ridge was interesting before, but now with him around, she couldn't wait to see what would happen next.

Lucy caught herself glancing into the mirror in the hall on her way into the kitchen.

He's already said he has no interest in a wife, she reminded herself. Still, she couldn't stop herself from humming. She had a feeling it was going to be a very good day.

"Morning, Tillie."

"Yes it is." The cook punched the dough with a raised brow. "What's gotten into you? Yesterday you were a bundle of nerves, and now…"

"Oh, nothing. Can't a girl just be happy?" Lucy grabbed an apron off the hook behind the closet door and quickly tied it around her waist. "How many do you think we've got this morning?"

"Ten. I'll bet Camilla doesn't have one."

Lucy opened the door and hurried through the cool morning breeze, crunching the snow beneath her feet, to the enclosed chicken coop where several hens sat as if they hadn't a care in the world.

"Hello, ladies. What do you have for me today?" She gathered up her apron to cradle the eggs as she checked beneath each of the eleven hens in the coop. Ten eggs.

How does she do it?

When she emerged from the pen, she spotted Lucas walking toward her from the barn. His hat rode low on his head and there was a swagger to his step.

"Feeling better?" She asked as he approached.

"I've never slept in a more comfortable bed." His eyes grew wide. "Excuse me, ma'am. I meant to say, I slept well. Thank you."

Lucy giggled. "I said the exact same thing when I arrived."

Lucas visibly relaxed.

"Liam likes quality and feels like everyone works better when they've had a good night's sleep. Even the beds in the bunkhouse were imported."

"How is my granddad this morning? Can I see him?"

"I don't see why not. The doctor is with him now, but you should be able to go up in a little while. However, I could use your help."

"I'm warning you now, I don't know anything about folding napkins."

Lucy laughed loudly. "Don't worry, if I need napkins folded, I'll teach you. Come on." She turned away from him and took a step toward the house. With no warning, her foot slipped out from beneath her and she squealed as she closed her eyes, waiting for impact.

"Whoa there, little lady." Lucas caught her under the arms before she could hit the ground.

She opened one eye and then the other. It wasn't exactly how she'd pictured being in his arms, but she had to admit, she liked being this close to him.

"Did I mention it's a little slick out here?" he said as he lifted her back to a standing position. She scrambled to gain her footing.

"Information that might have been helpful a few moments ago," she retorted with a smile.

"Here. Allow me." He removed his hat and turned it upside down. "May I?" he asked, pointing to her apron.

She opened the smock enough that he could collect the eggs and place them into his hat.

"Shall we?" He took a step.

Slick. Down he went.

Brewster's bark sounded from the nearby barn.

"We're okay," he said, holding the hat with the eggs in the air. "We're okay."

The border collie came running from around the side of the outbuildings and immediately started licking Lucas's face.

She looked down and couldn't help the giggle that escaped. She'd never seen a grown man fall flat on his behind before and the dog's enthusiasm added to the humorous scene.

"A little help, please."

Lucy snorted as she took his hat and bent down to help him up from the ground.

"Did I mention it's a little slick out here?" he repeated his earlier question with a laugh as he stood up and brushed the snow from his denims. "How are you, Brew?" he asked as he rubbed the back of the collie's head and ears. He smiled at Lucy, took his hat and cradled it in his arm, then reached out and took her hand in his.

Lucy forced herself to breathe. His touch sent tingles up her arm and filled her chest with a substance lighter than air.

Together, they took a step forward, then another, until they'd gingerly made their way to the back entrance with Brewster happily bringing up the rear.

"I think we're safe now," she said, unable to keep the chuckle from her voice.

Lucas released her hand to open the door. "After you," he said with a wink.

She stepped inside and showed him the bowl in the sink where he could put the eggs.

"Oh, no you don't." Tillie marched from behind the counter and led Brewster back outside, then dusted off her hands and looked up at Lucy. "How many?" she asked as she broke off another section of dough and added the rolled ball to the pan without missing a beat.

"Ten."

The plump cook grunted in satisfaction. "Now, I need those boxes."

"Oh, yes, we were just heading up for them." Lucy untied her apron and returned it to the hook on the other side of the pantry, then looked up at him. "We have to go up into the attic."

She showed him through the house, smiling at how wide his eyes grew when he realized there was an indoor privy with an extensive adjoining room for bathing. They passed by the library, the formal dining area, and the staircase on the far side of the house.

They climbed two flights of stairs before they reached the small door leading up to the attic.

"They're just in here." She stepped into the garret and climbed the few steps that led up to the main floor. The musty smell of memories long forgotten welcomed them.

Several boxes and dusty crates were stacked along the perimeter of the spacious room, offset only by a few pieces of old furniture and a child's rocking horse.

"Looks like a bunch of old junk. Why would Granddad keep it?" Lucas ran his finger across the top of the timeworn desk, leaving a trail where he'd wiped away the thick layer of dust.

A large casement window, thick with dirt and cobwebs, caught Lucy's attention. She trod across the creaky wooden floor and wiped a small section of grime from the glass. The view looked out over a far pasture where the horses could be seen running through and playing in the fresh snow. She jiggled the operator handle, but it wouldn't budge.

"Let me try."

She turned and stood, nearly crashing into the broad expanse of Lucas's chest. She looked up, her mouth suddenly dry.

"I'm sorry, I…" she couldn't finish her thought as her gaze turned to his mouth as it slowly descended toward her. She bit her bottom lip and closed her eyes. Waiting.

"I think it just needed a little nudge."

A wisp of cool air rose up her back until it caressed the bare skin at her neck. Her lashes fluttered open and she found herself, back pressed against the inside window sill, mere inches from Lucas's large form.

"It's a nice view." He took a step backward, away from her, a grin spread across his face as he shoved his hands into his pockets, exhaling heavily. He locked eyes with her for a moment, then turned to glance over the rest of the attic.

Lucy's heart beat with incessant rhythm and she brought a hand to her throat, playing with the lined edge of her dress there. She managed to smile back at him, but could not force herself to move.

He laughed as he strolled along the walls of boxes.

"What's this?" He pointed at one of the crates. It looked more like an old traveling case. 'Gabe Deardon' was clearly stenciled on the side. "I think it belonged to my father."

The air in the attic had grown nippy, so Lucy turned enough that she could crank the window shut.

Lucas tried to pull the trunk out from beneath a few boxes that had been stacked on top, but when he yanked on the handle, it came apart and he flew backward into the old desk and knocked a stack of papers out of one of the cupboards. He shook his hand as if he'd hurt himself in the process.

"Are you all right?" Lucy found her feet and made her way over to him, stopping to gather the stray papers and letters that had scattered on the floor. She quickly picked them up and shoved them into one of the slots on the desk.

"Fine. It just smarted a little." One by one, he took the boxes from on top and set them on the ground until the worn, brown trunk was exposed. He carefully pulled it from its resting spot and set it on a small end table next to a torn fainting couch and sat down.

"I imagine there are a lot of things up here that belonged to your father," Lucy said, scanning the rest of the items that had been stored. Several looked promising, but she feared her curiosity would get the better of her and they would spend the rest of the day looking through these old things.

"What of *your* father? How did you come to be at Whisper Ridge?" Lucas asked as he fiddled with the latch on the trunk.

"My father is a very busy businessman in New York, increasingly so since my mother passed a few years ago."

"I'm sorry for your loss."

"Me too. She was a wonderful, kind, and very beautiful woman."

"Like her daughter." Lucas smiled and warmth spread throughout Lucy's body.

"Once my father remarried, I spent much of my time looking after his new wife's three *darling* children." She was careful to keep the sarcasm from seeping into her voice. Truth was, the children had been quite a challenge for her and while she'd yearned for her father's affections, it had soon become apparent that what love he'd once had for her had died along with her mother. She'd become nothing more to him than a nanny for his new children.

The latch gave way and Lucas carefully lifted the lid to the trunk.

"And you decided the fresh Montana air would do you some good?" He pulled her from her unfortunate memories.

"That's a story for another day." She didn't want to tell him how she'd travelled across the country as a hopeful bride, only to be rejected and stranded in a new place at the mercy of his grandfather with nothing more than a trunk full of unrealized dreams. She nodded toward the open case.

Lucas pulled out a small, cinched leather bag with an 'L' carved into one side. He ran his fingers over the engraving.

"My marbles," he whispered, closing his fist over the pouch. He pulled out a slingshot, a wooden stagecoach, and a bilbo catcher. "Granddad kept all of these things?" His voice was quiet and a sense of nostalgia immediately filled every corner of the room.

"Who is this?" Lucy reached into the trunk and pulled out a photograph. "She's very pretty."

"On the outside maybe," Lucas scoffed as he continued to dig through the other items in the trunk. "I don't believe it."

Lucy returned the photograph to the trunk, but couldn't help wonder if it was his mother—the one who'd abandoned her husband and small children.

"What?"

He held up an almost new copy of Dumas's *Count of Monte Cristo.*

"It was Henry's," his said as he flipped through the pages. "Look, he's even made notes in some of the margins." He opened to a page where pencil scribbles dictated the thoughts of its reader. "Do you think Granddad would mind if I kept this?"

"I think Liam would be happy you found it."

He closed the trunk and stood up.

"I hope so. Henry would have liked that we found it." He placed the book in the back band of his trousers beneath his belt. "Now, I believe we had some boxes to collect."

CHAPTER ELEVEN

Lucy pointed to the empty crates in the corner, but as she passed the desk, her eye was drawn to one of the letters she had picked up from the ground, sitting cockeyed from the rest. She reached out and pulled the yellowed envelope from the disheveled stack and a photograph slipped out. As she bent down to pick it up, she turned the envelope over to inspect the writing.

Whittemore
New York

Her family's name, on her mother's side. She flipped the photograph over. There, staring back at her, was the image of her grandparents, her mother with a fellow she didn't recognize, and a much younger Liam Deardon holding a little girl. Her. She reached for the desk to support herself and felt around for the narrow chair, unwilling to take her eyes from the photograph.

Impossible!

She quickly pulled the letter from the envelope and scanned the contents.

March 7, 1843

Dear Mr. Liam Deardon,

Words cannot express the deep gratitude and respect I have for you. For a man of your position and power, it would have been easy to walk away after my wife's father, Mr. Joseph Whittemore, died unexpectedly, but you honored the promise you made to watch over and keep his family safe. I know, firsthand, the great lengths you went to in order to secure Claire a husband worthy of her. To this day, I am unsure that I could ever be as much as she deserves, but I love her and have cherished every moment we have spent together. I am forever grateful for the trust you placed in me.

I regret to inform you that I have taken ill and can no longer be the protector and provider I once was. The doctors tell me I will not live to see our precious baby girl's third birthday. I ask in earnest that you continue to watch over my beloved Claire and our little Lucy after I am gone. They mean more to me than life itself. Please let them know how very much I loved them. I know it is unfair of me to place this burden on your shoulders, but you are the only one I trust to see it through. Thank you.

Sincerely,

Adam Prescott

Lucy reread a portion of the letter over and over, unable to fathom the truth of its contents.

…our little Lucy

…our little Lucy

"…our little Lucy," she said aloud.

It can't be.

"What was that?" Lucas asked, coming to stand behind her. He pointed to the signature. "Do you know him? Adam Prescott?"

"I think…" She shook her head in disbelief. "I think he was my father."

"But I thought—"

"I have to go." She jumped to her feet, the letter clutched to her chest, and picked up her skirt as she ran down the attic steps and out the small door toward Liam's quarters.

"Who is Adam Prescott?" Lucy asked, gasping for air as she burst through the door to Liam's room.

He sat in a chair at the small table next to the hearth, overlooking the north pasture where the horses still frolicked. He still looked weak, but she needed answers.

She tossed the letters and the single photograph she'd discovered in the attic onto Liam's lap. "Who is Adam Prescott?" she asked again, more quietly this time.

He gave a resigned chuckle. "Come sit, Lucy." He pointed to a chair opposite him, picked up the old photograph, and rested his wrists on the table, caressing the picture.

"Your grandfather, Joseph, and I grew up in the same little town back East where we did everything together. We were inseparable, Joe and I. Even as we got older, we worked the same jobs, attended the same college, and courted the same girls." Liam set the photograph down on the table and looked at Lucy.

She leaned forward like a child might upon hearing a tale of adventure being recounted in great detail.

Cough.

"One day, a little over a year before you were born, a young painter by the name of Samuel Morse approached us and told of an electrical instrument he was working on that could transmit messages over a wire that would allow folks to communicate quickly with others in distant towns."

"The telegraph." It would explain how Liam had his own personal telegraph in his study.

"Yes. Joe and I were intrigued and pooled some of our substantial funds to invest in Morse's vision. Well, your grandfather died before that dream was realized, but not before I promised him that I would always take care of his family."

"And Adam Prescott?" Lucy stood up, too anxious to sit, and moved over next to the window.

"Adam was one of many prospective suitors who wanted Claire's hand in marriage. He was educated and refined with a good standing in society, but it was not his wealth and status that impressed me, but his strong character and unfailing kindness toward others. I knew he would do right by your mother."

"So, Adam Prescott is…" She needed to hear him say it.

"Your father."

Lucy closed her eyes. A weight lifted from her chest and she knew that it was true. She'd had a father who'd loved her 'more than life itself.' She just believed it about the wrong man.

"And Gerald Russell?"

Lucy'd had a pleasant childhood. The man she'd grown up knowing as her father had never been cruel or harsh in any way, and had always provided for her needs, but there had always been some intangible thing standing in the way of the relationship she'd hoped they would have.

"By the time Aaron's letter reached me, more than a month's time had come and gone." Liam got to his feet, and joined her at the window.

Cough. Cough.

"I sent an immediate response by courier, requesting to have Claire come here, to Whisper Ridge, but never heard a word."

Lucy turned to look up at Liam. Dark circles draped his eyes.

"You invited us to come live with you?"

"Yes. I had a promise to keep."

She turned back to look out the window. Lucas had captured the attention of his horse in the pasture below and proceeded to saddle him. He led the unique chestnut gelding into the corral and mounted. He trotted around the perimeter of the enclosure for a bit, then the rider disappeared from view. She scanned the corral, but there was no sign of him on the ground and instinctively she moved closer to the pane of glass.

Seconds passed and he was again astride his horse. She watched more closely as he rode a short spurt, and then dismounted at a run. He'd repeated his exercise a few times, adding a new little trick with each stint, before she realized Liam was watching her, not his grandson.

"He's a good man, you know."

Lucy glanced over her shoulder at him. She knew she should let him rest, but it was as if her whole life was being unfolded before her eyes and for the first time, she had a place where she felt like she belonged.

Cough. Cough.

"You should rest. Build up your strength so that you can watch the tournament tomorrow." Lucy guided him back to the large, four poster bed and pulled back the bedcoverings. She stoked the fire in the hearth and then leaned over and kissed her benefactor on the forehead. "*You* are a good man, Liam Deardon."

"I never stopped trying, you know." He grabbed ahold of her hand. "For years, I sent out letters, hoping to find what may have happened to young Claire and her child, but it wasn't until I received a short post from your stepfather that I learned of your whereabouts."

"He told you about my advertisement."

"Yes. And I knew I had to do for you what I'd done for your mother all those years ago."

"You've done more for me than you will ever know. And I will find my true love. I don't need your meddling to do it."

"Lucas is the man for you, Lucy girl. I know it."

Heat rushed to her cheeks and she smiled at the thought of him.

"Maybe, but—"

"You know it too." Liam shot up, looking more spry than she'd seen him since he'd returned. "You love him."

"How can I love a man I've only just met?" She crossed the room, picked up the pitcher of water, and poured him a glass.

"When it's right, you just know, lass."

"Shhh…" she glanced at the open door to make sure no one was listening. "Don't you try your brogue on me. It won't work. And you just keep those fancy notions to yourself, Mr. Deardon."

"Aye, lassie, but take my word, there'll be a weddin' here before spring." His impersonation of the accent was as good as any Scot's she'd ever heard.

She glanced out the window again.

Not if Lucas has anything to say about it.

CHAPTER TWELVE

A good ride was just what Lucas needed to get the charming Lucy Russell out of his mind. He pulled his tack down off the hook in the barn and carried it out to the pasture gate where he'd let Adonis out to run with the other horses this morning.

If he wasn't careful, he just might find himself falling for the light-haired beauty. There was something about her that threatened everything he believed about not being ready to get married and if he didn't stop thinking about her…well, he was playing a very dangerous game. It had taken everything he had to keep himself from going after her when she'd bolted from the attic. Something she'd found had upset her, but he was the last person who should comfort her. Instead, he'd just grabbed the empty crates and delivered them downstairs to Tillie in the kitchen.

Lucas climbed up onto the bottom rung of the gate, whistled loudly, and waited, scanning the immense pasture for any sign of the chestnut Quarter Horse with his exceptional cream-colored mane.

Brewster sprang from his hiding place under the porch

and happily joined Lucas at the gate, his tail wagging happily.

"Good boy," Lucas said, vigorously rubbing the dog behind the ears. "Where'd he go, Brew, huh?" His brother's would poke fun if they heard how he spoke to the pup.

The crisp whinny of his horse pulled Lucas back into a standing position and he smiled as Adonis cantered toward him. They'd worked on several tricks before they'd left home, but it had been a while and with the unfamiliar surroundings, he had been unsure whether or not the gelding would recognize the call.

After saddling his horse, Lucas led Adonis into the empty corral and mounted. His shoulder was a little stiff, but felt strong enough to practice a few tricks. He kissed the air, nudging the horse from a walk, to a trot, and then a light canter. They circled the corral a few times before he slid off the saddle to one side, holding himself tight against the side of the horse. A few seconds later, he pulled himself back up into the seat and continued at an even pace. The unusually warm sun peeked out from behind a billowing streak of cotton in an otherwise cloudless sky, but the melting snow didn't seem to bother the gelding in the slightest.

Lucas took a deep breath and dismounted, the horse still at a full gait. As Adonis rounded the corral again, he stepped in sync with the horse, grabbed ahold of the reins and pulled himself back up into the saddle. He drew back on the reins and stopped.

Several large targets made of round coiled straw mats sat perched on wooden easels at various distances. The painted cloths had yet to be strung over them for the tournament.

He dismounted, pulling a handful of dried apple slices he'd swiped from the kitchen while Tillie wasn't looking, and fed them to Adonis. "Good practice, Donnie," he said, rubbing his neck. He led the horse from the corral, removed the saddle, and released him back out into the pasture again with the other horses.

If tomorrow was this Deardon Thanksgiving tournament, he figured he'd probably best not do anything that could reinjure the shoulder. He carried the saddle, blanket, and tack back to the barn and strung it up on the hook he'd been given.

"I'm sorry I left you alone in the attic."

Lucas whipped around to see Lucy leaning against the barn door. A halo of light shone round her face as the sun lit the edges of her hair. She was striking.

"Is everything all right?" he asked hesitantly.

"Better than all right," she said with a smile. "Let's just say I got a lot of answers to questions I didn't know I had."

"Okay."

"Come on. Liam said I need to show you around the place. We can do that while we check that everything is in place for tomorrow."

"So, a log toss, an archery match, a stick pull, leg wrestling, and a riding course."

"Yes."

"How many are coming?" he asked as they reached the stables, his boots crunching the ground beneath him.

"Nine Deardon competitors, if you take Liam's place, and then a few of the hands are also given the opportunity to compete. Only those over sixteen are allowed to participate—which Sam's youngest is still bitter about—he's only fourteen—and the winner gets a hefty prize."

Sam was his father's youngest brother. Back home, Lucas had nearly forgotten he had a whole family outside of Oregon—except for Aunt Leah and her family in Kansas. None of them could forget her. He liked the idea of having a big family.

"Granddad still participates in these events?"

"Not this year, for obvious reasons." Lucy swung open the doors and stepped inside of the stable. "We'll need the sleigh hitched please, Jake," she told the stable hand, who placed his shovel against the wall, nodded, and disappeared around the corner of an empty stall.

"Who are the others?"

"You know Hank and Sam." She stopped and turned to look at him. "You *do* know Hank and Sam, right?"

"I know they're my uncles, but I haven't seen them in years."

Lucy's eyes closed into discerning slits and she shook her head. "Their ranches aren't too far from here. They are each bringing their families. Your Aunt Leah sent her regrets for this year. It's just too long of a trek from Kansas to Montana with her little ones. Did you know she's got eight children? Eight! You Deardons certainly don't do anything small."

Lucas laughed. "How do you know so much about my family?"

"I'm sorry. You must think me entirely improper. I've only been here a month, but Liam likes to talk and I listen. When you're helping to plan an event as big as the Deardon tournament, you learn a few things."

Wait, did she said nine competitors?

Her words just hit him and suddenly, he wasn't at all sure he was prepared to meet so many new relatives who might not hold his father in the highest esteem. When he'd thought about coming out to see his granddad, he'd tried to remember anything he could about Uncle Hank and Uncle Samuel. Jonah and Noah had had a few stories, but he'd been so young when they'd left that he didn't remember anything about them or their children. Aunt Leah, however, had made a point to write often and he and his brothers had spent time at Redbourne Ranch after their mama left. Aunt Leah had wanted to make sure they'd had some female influence in their lives so they didn't turn into a bunch of scroungy backwoodsmen in the wilds of Oregon.

"Ready?" Lucy looked up at Lucas expectantly.

He wasn't sure where they were headed. How big could Whisper Ridge possibly be? But, he wanted to learn as much as he could about the tournament tomorrow. That way he would be prepared for what awaited him. So, if accompanying Miss Russell for an early afternoon ride was going to provide that, who was he to argue?

"Mr. Deardon," she said, pulling him from his thoughts. "Are you ready?" she repeated.

"When you are."

CHAPTER THIRTEEN

The double doors of the stable groaned in protest as they opened. She turned to say something to Liam's grandson, but froze when her face nearly met with his broad chest.

Good heavens.

Lucy could hardly breathe. Being so close to Lucas Deardon had become all too familiar too quickly. She was sure they violated several rules of propriety, not that she minded much here or in the attic. She was quickly learning that the rules that governed society in New York were not the same here. Her cheeks warmed at the thought.

When Lucas had first arrived at the ranch, she'd not known what to make of him, but after seeing how confidently he handled himself under pressure, and the tenderness he'd displayed with his grandfather, she'd had to stop herself on more than one occasion from dreaming of those thick arms wrapped around her.

Stop it right now, Lucy Russell.

She took a step away from him. Still, she couldn't help but wonder what it would have been like had a man like Lucas Deardon requested the mail-order-bride instead of Gilroy

Hearn.

"The sleigh is ready, Miss Lucy." Jake handed her down a large cozy blanket for the ride, then he pulled the horses out into the yard and jumped down.

"Thanks, Jake. We won't be out too long." She told him, though she guessed Lucas wouldn't have a problem unhitching the sleigh when they returned. The light afternoon breeze blew the hair away from Lucy's face, allowing the sunlight to warm her skin. It felt good.

"Shall we?" she asked Lucas as they made their way to the front of the sled. The snow had already started to melt, unusual for this time of year, but the chill still nesting in the air promised the crystal-topped ground would be around for a while. In her experience, an Indian summer was generally followed by the harshest of winter seasons and she shivered at the thought.

Lucas slipped his hands around her waist and lifted her effortlessly up onto the bench. His touch sent gooseflesh cascading down her arms.

"So, where are we going?"

This was a mistake. If she cared anything about protecting her heart, she would get down off the sleigh and as far away from Lucas as possible.

"To show you Whisper Ridge."

"Aren't we already here?"

"Take a look out, as far as you can see, in every direction."

Lucas looked around him and although the stables blocked his view to the south, she saw the same wonder in his eyes as she'd felt when she'd first arrived and learned of the immensity of the ranch.

"*That* is Whisper Ridge. All of it. Hi-yah!" she called out to her two favorite draft horses.

Before they could even get out of the main gate, sleigh bells jingled in the distance. It had to be Hank. She'd sent Denver out to his place early this morning and then to Sam's to inform them both about what had happened with their father.

Hank and his oldest son, Seth, emerged through a small thicket of pines and hastily crossed the wide bridge separating the homesteads.

"We were just on our way to see you." Lucy said as Hank pulled up next to her.

"Mara had one of those feelings last night that something was wrong." Hank's eyes shot to Lucas and back to her. He raised his gun heavenward, lifted the fore-end into the air, and cocked it. "When Denver showed up this morning, we came as soon as we could get away. What's going on, Lucy?"

"I'm glad to see you," Lucy said, daring a glance at the man seated next to her.

"Your father is going to be unable to participate in the games tomorrow and Lucas is going to take his place."

"What's wrong with Dad?" Hank asked, raising a brow. "I'm sorry, who are you?" he asked, not waiting for the first question to be answered. He clutched the rifle menacingly, fixing his gaze on Lucas.

"There was an accident with the water tower. A stampede knocked out the braces and the tower fell. Granddad's up in his room resting. Doctor's orders. I'm Lucas, by the way. Lucas Deardon," he said, standing up and leaning over with his hand extended.

Hank ignored it, but he dropped his gun to his side.

"I'm Seth. Deardon," the younger man said with a grin as he jumped down off his sleigh.

Lucas climbed down to meet him.

Hank didn't say a word, but slapped the reins and drove up next to the stables where he handed the straps to Jake.

Seth's brows scrunched together as he took Lucas's proffered hand. "Uncle Gabe's kid, right?"

"Yes, sir."

"What's all this 'sir' nonsense? We're cousins. Family."

Seth pulled Lucas into stiff hug, then followed Lucas's eyes to Hank's retreating form. "Don't mind him. He's still mad at your dad for leaving. Even after all these years." Seth looked up at Lucy, who still sat on the wagon bench. "I'm sorry, were you two headed somewhere?"

Lucy felt the color rush into her cheeks. "Not anymore. It can wait. I'm sure Lucas would like the chance to get to know you. Why don't we head back up to the house?" She drove the sleigh back to the barn. "I told you we wouldn't be gone long," she said, smiling at Jake.

She was glad to see Lucas and Seth already getting along so well. They hadn't stopped talking to each other as they followed her on foot. Lucas walked up to the side of the sled and reached up to help her down. She smiled at him and allowed him to lower her to the ground.

"Your grandfather's fever has broken, but it'll be a while before he'll be back to his old self."

The silence that followed as Seth looked between her and Lucas put Lucy at a loss for words and she folded her lips together, careful to avoid the man's eyes.

"I'm sure there's a story here, but it'll keep. For now," Seth said, a grin spread across his face as he patted Lucas on the shoulder. "Glad to have you back, cousin."

There *was* a story, but the ending had yet to be written.

Mrs. Lucas Deardon. The name had promise. After all, it couldn't be a coincidence that both of their names started with the same few letters. She might have thought it fate. If she believed in such things. It wasn't like her to entertain such silly notions, but he affected her more than she cared to admit.

"You staying long?" Seth asked.

Lucy glanced over at Lucas, attempting to keep the hope from her eyes. With several eligible Deardon men surrounding her at any given moment, this was the first time she'd found herself wanting, hoping, to be noticed.

She held her breath, waiting for him to answer.

How long are you staying? She asked silently, as if by thinking the question, would will him to respond more quickly.

"That...," he said as he stole a glance at her, "has yet to be determined."

CHAPTER FOURTEEN

Thanksgiving Day

DING! CLANG! DING! CLANG! DING!

Lucas shot up out of his bed and scrambled to his feet, his heart pounding wildly in his chest as he swiftly collected his rifle from the side of the nightstand next to his bed.

"Whoa, slow down there, partner." His cousin, Seth, broke out with a huge guffaw, nearly bent over with laughter, a metal meal triangle clutched in his hands.

"I'm sorry," Seth said with a snicker, "did we wake you?"

Lucas glanced at the other culprit leaning up against the vanity dresser.

"I'm Daniel," the dark-haired stranger said with a smirk and a wave. "Sam's oldest."

Lucas stepped back, wondering if his mind was playing tricks on him. If he didn't know any better, he would have thought it was Henry. There was no doubt they were related. He had to give his cousins credit. Generally, this kind of tomfoolery was his doing at home, but he'd never been on the receiving end.

"You're lucky I didn't kill you."

"Eh, you're a Deardon. Instincts are what keep us alive around here. You weren't going to shoot us. Come on." Seth threw the denims Lucas had left draped over the chair last night in his face. "We eat breakfast early on tournament day."

"I just want to check in on Granddad this morning and then I'll be down."

"It *is* odd to see him weak and so tired looking, but you'll find out he can't sit still for long. He's already eaten his breakfast and is working on something with Mr. Tacy in the study."

With all these new names and faces, Lucas was having a hard time keeping track of everyone. He had no idea who Mr. Tacy was, but after seeing the exhaustion in his granddad's eyes yesterday, it worried Lucas that he wasn't resting as ordered.

"Does Miss Russell know he's up?" Lucas wanted to ask his cousins how Lucy had come to be on the ranch, but thought better of it. He was sure he'd learn soon enough.

"Lucy? I'm sure she does. She knows everything that goes on around here. It's only a matter of time before granddad agrees to let one of us marry the girl," Daniel said just before disappearing out the door.

Lucas tilted his head and squinted his eyes as he pondered that last statement. His granddad had practically insisted on him marrying the woman. If there had been plenty of Deardon men already willing to do so, why had he chosen Lucas for the…opportunity?

His heart skipped a beat at the thought, but he ignored the sensation. It was Noah's turn to get married. Lucas chided himself for not volunteering to be the one to go to Markham's and learn the cattle trade. Then, maybe granddad would have insisted that Noah marry Lucy.

The more he thought about it, the more he realized that he didn't like the idea of his brother marrying her, or anyone else for that matter. There was something about Lucy that almost made him forget his reasons for saying no. Not only was she beautiful, but she was smart and had a kind heart.

It didn't take long to shrug into his britches and join the rest of his family down in the kitchen for food. The over-sized table was covered with steaming plates piled high with flapjacks, eggs, an assortment of meats, and a large pot of what looked to be creamed porridge. It had been a long time since he'd seen this amount of food at breakfast time. Back home, they were lucky to have day-old biscuits and jerky with fresh milk.

When he stepped into the room, it fell silent and several pairs of eyes turned to look at him. Some were faces he now recognized, but others were still unfamiliar.

The competitors, he guessed. However, he didn't see Uncle Hank or Sam among them.

"Hello," Lucas waved awkwardly.

Seth shoved a plate of food into his hand and Lucas followed him to an open seat at the table in front of the door. He glanced out the window. Water dripped from the fence where the brightly shining sun continued to melt the snow. If it weren't for the ground covered in a blanket of white, he would have believed it a fresh spring morning.

"Well, you boys ready to compete?" A firm hand warmed Lucas's shoulder as his granddad came up behind him. Liam squeezed, however lightly. He bent over to Lucas's ear. "How's the shoulder today?" he asked.

Surprised, Lucas turned to look at him and his granddad winked.

"Good, thank you." He stood to allow Liam a place to sit, then leaned with one foot against the wall, next to the door, holding his plate. As he scooped a spoonful of food into his mouth, he watched how easily his granddad interacted with the others.

Now, it's my turn to get to know him, he thought with a smile.

At first glance, the older man seemed to be feeling better, but despite his easy smile, there was something in his face, in his eyes, that still betrayed his weariness.

The kitchen door opened. Before Lucas could move out of the way, Lucy stepped inside, brushing wet droplets from her coat all over him.

Runoff from the roof, he gathered.

"Denver assures me that the cloth targets have been secured to the round straw boards and the ring in the barn has been swept and readied for the leg wrestling matches." She brushed wet tendrils out of her face. When she glanced up, her eyes locked with Lucas's.

"Oh, excuse me," she said with an expression that told Lucas she'd just seen him.

Lucas was taken aback by the feelings she evoked in him. He'd been tempted by several beautiful women, but all of them paled in comparison to her. Even with wet hair and her nose red from the cold, she was beautiful.

I'm not getting married. I'm not getting married. Who was he trying to convince?

A different voice interrupted his thoughts as Lucas could hear Emma's constant reminders of how a gentleman should treat a lady, but before he could get his body to cooperate with his mind, his granddad prodded him.

"Well, aren't you going to help her with her coat, son?" Liam asked as he turned around and looked at Lucas.

He set his plate down on the table and reached out to her. "Yes, sir." He didn't need any more encouragement. Being a gentleman didn't require any kind of commitment.

"May I?" he asked.

Lucy looked around at the table, color flooding her cheeks, but she allowed him to remove the covering.

"Thank you," she said as he handed it back to her. "I've had Jake pull two of your stuffed chairs out onto the porch where you will have a wonderful view of the outdoor events,

Liam," she told his grandfather.

Lucas appreciated the warm pink glow that now highlighted her face.

"...and then we'll move them into the barn where you can be close enough to watch the indoor events and feel like you're a part of it all.

"I would feel like I was a part of it if I was participating," he grumbled. "You know I'm not one for sitting on my hind end watchin' like a..."

"Like a what?" Her hands were on her hips and one eyebrow cocked.

Lucas noticed that all the men seated at the table had suddenly become very interested in the food in front of them, their heads bent low and staring into their dishes.

"Like a woman?" She opened her mouth as if to say more, but closed it again and smiled.

"Ah," Granddad waved his hand flippantly in the air, "you know what I mean."

Lucy smiled and kissed the top of his head. "Good luck, gentlemen. The festivities will begin in half an hour," she said before retreating to the other room.

Granddad looked up at Lucas, raised a brow, and then turned to everyone at the table. "Which one of you boys is going to marry that girl?" he asked.

Lucas laughed.

Every hand at that table went into the air and another twinge of jealousy curdled in Lucas's stomach at the thought of anyone else gaining her favor. His granddad turned and looked at him again. Waiting. Apparently, he had not been joking. After a few moments of awkward silence, Lucas raised his hand.

"It's settled." Liam tapped the table with a satisfied grunt. "The unmarried man with the highest points in the tournament will take her hand."

Marriage? Lucas swallowed. *What have I done? Court her?*

Yes. Get to know her? Absolutely. But, marry her? With a deep breath, he closed his eyes and accepted what his heart had known all along. He couldn't let her marry somebody else when he was already in love with her.

Sorry, Noah. It looks like I may be cutting in line.

CHAPTER FIFTEEN

Lucy stood pressed up against the outside wall of the kitchen, listening to Liam offer her up as a prize to all of his grandsons over the age of sixteen. She was mortified. After forging her way west with a promise that she would be given a home and companion, Gilroy Hearn had left her standing alone in the middle of the road in Thistleberry, Montana.

It was an experience she didn't care to repeat. Liam Deardon saved her that day, and she owed him everything. However, she didn't want to marry just any Deardon man, she wanted to marry Lucas. But he'd made it perfectly clear that he had no desire to marry anyone.

Liam's question still lingered in the air and she couldn't help but to peek around the wall. Her breath caught in her chest and her heart leapt when she saw six Deardon men with their hands in the air. Then, the seventh. Lucas raised his hand. She pulled back against the wall, her hand against her chest, willing her heart to calm.

He raised his hand? Why did he raise his hand?

Each of the Deardon men was handsome in his own right

and all had wealth enough to provide for her and any children that might come along—her cheeks heated at that thought—but until yesterday, she hadn't considered any of them as a potential spouse. They were all very young and felt like siblings more than suitors.

She darted a glance around the corner and caught another glimpse of Lucas, still leaning against the wall, staring down at the floor, and a smile worked its way onto her lips. She raised a hand to touch them.

Marriage! She bit her bottom lip, her hands clasped at her chin. Apparently, he'd changed his mind. The only thing that could ruin this day was if someone other than Lucas won.

Several of the men gathered around the stables. Horses, new to Whisper Ridge, had been brought in from neighboring ranches to keep the competition fair. Sticks of various lengths had been put into a cup and each participant was to draw to determine the order they would select their mounts for the course.

Lucy pulled the warm quilted blanket up around Liam's shoulders. "You'll catch a chill out here if you're not careful."

"Aw, Lucy, it's warmer right now than it's been in weeks. The fresh air will do us both some good. Now, stop your fussin' and sit down!"

For as much as Liam grumbled at her, he wasn't unreasonable. She understood how hard it was for him to sit back and watch, but as much as he would hate to admit it, she believed that he knew he just wasn't up for the physical challenge.

He was tired. Dark circles fell like shadows beneath his eyes and his cheeks appeared sunken. Hollow. His normally tanned skin had a greyish tinge and she worried that he'd already overdone himself.

"They've all mounted," Liam said excitedly, pointing to the riders as they headed for the starting point.

While it was still difficult for her to tell some of the breeds apart, Lucy looked up to see Lucas astride a beautiful, and unmistakable, buckskin mare. Some of the others had horses much larger in stature than his, but poor Daniel appeared to have chosen the short stick, as his mount didn't look any bigger or well-bred than a pack mule. Not that she really knew enough about horses to tell the difference, to Liam's chagrin.

Daniel didn't look any too pleased.

The racing trail had been set off with flagged markers staked at intervals extending a good distance around the property where there were unobstructed views from the front porch. With nary a breeze, it was hard to believe that such a nasty storm had passed through the day before yesterday. The snow had started to melt, but Lucy enjoyed the feel of the sun as it warmed her face.

"You are a better woman than I, Lucy Russell." Hank's wife, Mara, stepped up onto the porch and sat down on the arm of Lucy's chair. "You sure you want to marry one from this brood?"

"For the chance to have you as a mother-in-law? Of course."

"Ahh…flattery. There's hope for you yet." Mara looked down at her and winked.

CRACK!

Smoke rose from the gun Alex held in the air, signaling the start of the race. A white spray of snow spread across the landscape as riders quickly made their way around each marker as they spanned the course. The horses had all been outfitted with special shoes built for gaining traction in the snow.

Lucy sat forward in her chair, fixing her eyes on the contestants. After all, she was supposed to have a life-changing stake in the outcome.

It didn't take long for the leaders to separate themselves

from the rest. Hank, Seth, and Sam rode neck to neck as they rounded the bend near the corral fence line and, to Lucy's delight, Lucas joined the foray at Sam's heels.

She held her breath. It wouldn't be long now before the first crossed the finish line.

As Hank and Sam leaned forward in their seats and rode toward the edge of the barn, Lucy's attention was caught by a shift in the snow on the roof. She glanced from the clump of snow threatening to fall, then back to the riders. She stood.

Just as the brothers reached the barn, the snow slipped from the top of the roof and dropped on top of their heads. Seth swerved out of the way, nearly running into Lucas's horse. Lucy brought a hand to her mouth. Lucas had disappeared from the saddle.

"Where'd he go?" Liam asked, moving to the edge of his seat.

Mara jumped up from the chair and rushed to the railing, looking toward the barn, where her husband had just been attacked by the roof's avalanche. When he and Sam both emerged, still in their saddles, Mara stepped back, her hand on her chest, and smiled.

Lucy scanned the ground, but Liam's estranged grandson was not anywhere to be seen. The empty horse still rode neck and neck with Seth's toward the finish line. As they approached the end, Lucas suddenly reappeared, lifting himself from the opposite side of his mount, and regained his place in the saddle, urging his horse faster.

"Whew." The audible sound of relief that came from Liam was palpable. "How'd he do that?" He leaned back against the back of the chair.

The younger of the Deardon boys stood on the ground in front of the porch and clapped heartily at Lucas's feat. Lucy, Liam, and Mara joined in.

Hank and Sam, trying to gain ground, came up quickly on Seth and Lucas's heels. They weren't going to let the win go easily. Snow dusted their jackets and filled the empty spaces between them and their saddles, but it didn't serve as a deterrent.

The picturesque backdrop, accompanied by the methodic rhythm of the horses' movements, slowed time as Lucy watched with anticipation for the man who would take an early lead in the tournament.

From her position on the porch, it was difficult to tell which horse had been first to cross—Seth's or Lucas's. Alex, who was considered the final judge for this tournament, bent down from her horse and whispered something to her youngest. He nodded.

Lucy watched him expectantly. He took the steps two at a time and with a quick gesture, motioned for Lucy to come closer. The fourteen-year-old was taller than her, so he bent down and cupped his hand around her ear, then leaned in.

"Seth was first. Lucas second. Then my dad and Uncle Hank tied for third," he whispered. Without waiting for a response, he jumped down off the porch and rejoined his brothers and cousins, who were now all congratulating the riders.

"Well?" Mara asked expectantly.

Lucy forced a smile. "Seth."

Mara squeezed her arm and skittered down the steps toward her son.

Lucy tried to squelch the disappointment that bubbled in her belly. Seth was a good man—handsome, strong, fun—but she was afraid that her heart had already been claimed by somebody else. Lucas. She sat back down in the overstuffed chair Jake had brought out for her. Liam placed his hand over hers.

"He is a good man, isn't he?"

"Yes, Seth has everything a woman could hope for."

"I wasn't talking about Seth."

Lucy looked at Liam. "How did you know?"

"I see it in your eyes every time you look at him." He coughed. "Don't worry. This day is not over yet. There are still four events. I have a feeling Gabe's boy can hold his own."

Lucy smiled.

I hope so.

CHAPTER SIXTEEN

"That was amazing," Seth said as he congratulated Lucas with a bear-like hug. "Where did you learn to ride like that?"

Lucas had never been more grateful for his ability to pull off a stunt in his life. He'd caught a glimpse of the snow crashing down from the barn's roof and had slipped off the horse to one side in time to avoid being knocked out of his saddle. Luckily, his good arm had been able to support most of his weight and he'd been able to regain the saddle with little effort.

"An old trick-rider showed me a few of his feats. I've practiced a few times."

"Well, you keep riding like that and maybe you'll win next year," Seth teased as he turned to his mother and picked her up off the ground and twirled her about.

Lucas looked up at the porch where Lucy sat in the chair next to his granddad. She smiled at him and he waved. He'd only lost the race by an inch, but he'd still lost. He tried to convince himself that it didn't matter. He barely knew Lucy, so why would he care if she married his cousin? At least she would have a good name and someone to take care of her.

Who am I kidding? I think I'm in love with her. I can't lose. I just can't.

"I've never lost at something I put my mind to and I'm not about to start now," he said quietly as he made his way to the stables with his mount. The buckskin had proven to be a good choice, but he was confident he would have won had he been able to ride Adonis.

You don't have anything to prove. Jonah's words echoed in Lucas's mind. Being the youngest, he'd often struggled with finding a place for himself back home and the idea of returning without purpose weighed heavily on him. Especially now, as they transitioned to cattle ranching, it was time for him to find where he belonged. Horses were his passion and he loved working with the mustangs. He'd seen plenty of opportunities here at Whisper Ridge just in the last twenty-four hours and knew he had everything to prove if he wanted to stay.

That last thought took him by surprise.

I want to stay.

After seeing to his horse, he joined the others outside where Aunt Alex had finished writing their placements on an over-sized slate chalkboard.

"Second place, Deardon. Not bad, for a first timer." Seth laughed and patted him on the shoulder.

"One event!" Lucas responded incredulously. "We've had one event." He snorted softly at how comfortable he already felt with the people who'd so graciously accepted him into their lives. He'd been a stranger a couple of days ago, and now, he was a part of the family.

Seth laughed again as he waved and disappeared into the small crowd of competitors and onlookers.

The next event was the caber toss and Lucas was more than a little nervous. He'd helped out a few times at the Whittaker place back in Oregon, throwing logs alongside some of the lumberjacks, and he understood all too well the strength it required. But to throw one for sport…he rubbed his arm just thinking about it. He flexed his hand a couple of times, then followed Seth to the meadow, where the snow had begun to melt into muddy puddles and sopping vegetation.

Several massive logs, much taller than Lucas had expected, had been laid out along the edges of the field. Because of his placement in the last event, he would be the second to last competitor to throw the caber.

Denver was up first. He walked out onto the field where the log had already been laid out for him. Uncle Hank lifted it from the far end and walked his way up the pole until it was standing up straight in front of the participant.

Lucas watched with interest as Denver leaned over and locked his hands, fingers intertwined around the pole. He lowered his hands in laddered movements until he was able to lift the log and get his hands underneath it without it tipping over. It appeared even taller when being held in the air. The foreman took a moment to steady himself before starting forward with small, quick steps.

Just when the caber looked as if it might fall from his hands, he plowed his feet into the ground and heaved the log forward. It didn't go far. Denver dropped his head, shaking it back and forth. Lucas guessed it landed maybe five feet from the man.

The next to step forward was no taller than Denver, but looked as if he weighed half as much. He followed the same basic steps as the first, but after he'd lifted the log into the air, it tumbled backward until it fell behind him.

This might be tougher than I thought.

When it was finally his turn, Lucas took a deep breath, walked out onto the field, and glanced up at the porch where his granddad sat watching. The old man tipped his imaginary hat with a nod. Lucas nodded back. Then his gaze fell to Lucy. She'd moved to one of the porch posts, leaning into and draping her arm around it. She captured her bottom lip in her teeth and then smiled at him in a way that put clouds beneath his feet.

Focus, Deardon! There was more than one thing at stake here—Lucy's hand and his grandfather's approval.

He'd always been a quick study, but his heart pounded so loudly he could hear it echoing in his head. Hank, who'd thrown the caber the farthest thus far, waited for his signal. Lucas breathed in and held it for a moment. Then released it slowly, closing his eyes to gain focus. He opened them and nodded at Hank. It only took a moment for his uncle to stand the log upright in front of him.

Lucas bent his knees and hunched over as he wrapped his hands around the pole like he'd seen all of the others do. He laced his fingers together, working to keep his breathing even and steady as his hands leapt down toward the bottom of the log. With one swift movement, he maneuvered his clutch beneath the beam and held it firmly against his shoulder, which, to his amazement, did not pain him.

He marked the spot in his mind where he would stop to throw the caber. He'd noted that the most successful of them had taken only a few steps before tossing. With another slow exhale, he blocked everything else from his mind, except the task at hand. One step. Two. Three. Lucas focused all of his strength into his hands and arms, and heaved the log, tossing it forward.

"Ahhhhhh!" He grabbed his shoulder, holding his breath, waiting for the caber to land. Finally, the tip hit the ground and the end he'd been holding tumbled over the top.

He bent in half, his shoulder now throbbing, and let out the air that had been trapped in his lungs. Screams, whoops, and hollers erupted from the group and in moments, the small crowd, made up mostly of his large family, surrounded him.

"Nicely done," Hank grunted the words, nodding curtly as he passed by.

Lucas stood up straight just in time for Seth to pick him

up and raise him into the air. "Whoop!" he hollered. "Now, how am I supposed to beat that?"

Lucas had never felt so excited and relieved at the same time.

"I have never seen anyone throw like that," Daniel said with a pat on his back. "You are full of surprises. Are you sure you've never done this before?"

Lucas groaned. His shoulder burned as if on fire.

"Not like this," Lucas said, grinding his teeth against the pain.

"You don't look so good," Seth told him as he placed a hand on each of Lucas's shoulders.

"Aaahhhh!" Lucas cried out again in agony, his good hand shooting instinctively to place pressure on the injured limb.

Lucas, Daniel, and Seth walked to the fence where the doctor already waited, Lucy by his side.

"Thanks, Doc," Lucas said through another groan. "I appreciate you being willing to come and take a look."

"Don't thank me. Thank Miss Lucy. She's the one who invited me to stay."

Lucas met her eyes, hoping his gratitude would show through.

"I could see something was wrong as soon as the log went into the air," she said apologetically.

"Is everything all right over here?" Liam had descended the porch steps and crossed the lawn to meet them at the fence. "Lucas, you all right, son?"

"I'll be fine. I think I just reinjured my shoulder."

"I knew it had been bothering you. How did you hurt it the first time?"

Lucas looked at his granddad, unsure he wanted to admit he'd been hurt doing the same thing that had gotten Henry killed. He looked down at his feet. "It dislocated when I was thrown from a wild mustang."

Liam laughed. Something Lucas had certainly not

expected. "Like father, like son."

Lucas scrunched his brows together.

"Eh, it's a tale for another time." Liam turned to the doc. "He gonna live?"

"Let's step into the house where I can get a good look at that shoulder, without turning you into a block of ice," Doc said with a smile, then turned to Liam. "If he's as stubborn as the rest of you Deardons, I have a feeling he'll do what it takes."

Lucas and the doc walked the short distance to the front porch steps leading into the parlor, followed by Lucy, Seth, and his grandfather. He hated all the fuss, but complied with the doctor's instructions. The warmth of the fire inside the house contrasted hugely with the cold weather.

"Off with 'em—the coat and shirt both."

Lucas didn't move. He'd already bandaged the shoulder in preparation for today and didn't feel like hearing how foolish it had been to compete with a known injury.

"Come on," the doc pressed.

Lucas raised his hands to the large buttons on the front of his coat with some difficulty. The pain was different this time. It didn't feel out of joint like it had before, but something was definitely wrong. He didn't have the time or the patience for another injury. There were still three events to go, and all of them would require the use of his arm.

"Oh, for heaven's sake." Lucy stepped forward and made quick work of the coat buttons, careful to avoid his gaze. She tossed the wool-lined jacket onto the couch and paused for only a moment before tackling the buttons of his shirt. Her fingers shook as she brushed his bare skin beneath the cloth.

Lucas sucked in at her touch. How was he supposed to focus now?

When the last button had been undone, Lucy finally glanced up and their eyes locked for one brief moment before she stepped away. He opened the shirt enough for Doc to see his bandages. Seeing the injured arm was apparently not enough for the doctor as he reached inside, pushing and prodding the shoulder and chest area, making his experienced assessment.

Granddad took a step forward and opened his mouth to say something, but his footing faltered and he stumbled.

"I think you need to sit for a bit, Liam," Doc said. "Lucy, maybe you should take him up to his room to rest."

"I am not going to be confined to my blasted bedroom. I'll just sit outside in the chair on the porch. I don't want to miss a thing. Achoo!" He turned to look at Lucas, pulling an old handkerchief from his pocket. "You gonna be all right?"

Lucas nodded.

Lucy draped his grandfather's arm over her shoulder and turned around.

"Here," Seth said as he stepped toward them, "let me help." He took their granddad's other arm and placed it over his shoulder.

Lucy glanced back at Lucas. Only her eyes showed above the width of the arm she carried and they locked with his.

I am going to marry that girl.

They opened the door and Lucas watched them through the wall of windows as Lucy and Seth helped his grandfather back into his chair and tucked the blankets up around him. Seth laughed at something she said and a heavy pit formed in Lucas's belly.

"Ow." Lucas rotated his arm, protesting against the manipulation of his muscles. "I'm fine, Doc. Really. Can you just rewrap it?"

Blasted shoulder.

"Certainly, you don't think you can continue to compete?"

"Don't have a choice, Doc. There's too much at stake." He looked back out at the porch, but both Lucy and Seth were gone.

"You really should let the shoulder rest. Your granddad's

got some clean linens in the closet just outside the study. I can make a sling that will help you to be more aware of the need to keep it still."

"I don't need a sling, I need something that will help brace it against the pain."

"Let's head on over and we'll see what we can do."

Lucas didn't take the time or make the effort to button his shirt. As they stepped into the entrance, Lucas caught another glimpse of his grandfather through the window.

"I'll meet you there," he said as he held a hand up to the doctor. He opened the door and strode over where Liam sat comfortably in his chair with a blanket wrapped up around him watching the other competitors as they chatted amongst themselves. He wasn't sure what he wanted to say, but acted on the feeling he needed to say something. When he'd first met the man, only a day or so ago he realized, his grandfather had seemed so much stronger. So full of life.

"Granddad," Lucas started. He hadn't expected to feel so much after such a short time.

Cough. Cough.

"How's that shoulder? Are you going to be able to participate in the archery event? It was always your daddy's favorite."

Gabe had always insisted that his sons learn how to use a bow as well as a rifle. Said it might save their lives one day. Lucas sat down in the seat next to his grandfather and leaned down, his elbow on his knee.

"I just wanted you to know how…how grateful I am that…"

"It's all right, son. I'm just so glad you're home." Liam patted his leg.

Home.

CHAPTER SEVENTEEN

"You've really made an impact on my granddad, Miss Lucy," Seth told her as he reached up into the top cabinet of the study armoire to retrieve his grandmother's salve. "I've never seen him take a liking to anyone as easily as he has to you. Except maybe Lucas."

Was that jealousy in his voice?

Seth Deardon was very handsome—standing well over six feet tall, dark hair, and strong chiseled features—and he was smart. His fun-loving nature endeared him to her, but she didn't feel the same draw to him as she did to Lucas. He was more like a brother than anything.

"My cousin really likes you too, you know."

"Which one?" she asked, full well understanding of whom he spoke. She smiled. "I know about the tournament, Seth. About all of it."

At first he looked as if he might deny it, but he smiled at her. "You know Granddad didn't mean any harm."

"I know."

"We all agreed to go along with it because he believes you and Lucas are perfect for each other."

"Then why did he want you all to agree that the winner would marry me?" She knew she should be nervous, but somehow she was completely at ease talking with him.

"There's nothing that'll win over a Deardon like a little friendly competition."

"You have to know I wouldn't marry a man just because he can ride a horse or shoot an arrow better than the others. I already had my attempt at marrying for the wrong reasons. Now, I'll only marry for the right ones."

"I know." Seth handed her the small tin canister. "And Granddad knows too."

She breathed a chuckle.

"What is so special about that salve, anyway?" she asked with interest. "To hear Liam speak of it, you would think it had some magical healing power."

Seth laughed.

"Most of us believe so." He smiled. "It's Grandma's concoction of rosemary leaves and peppermint mixed with a few other things. She and Aunt Leah were the only ones to ever get it right. Granddad's real stingy with it as this is the last of the poultice and Aunt Leah doesn't make it up here very often to make more."

She opened the container, a deliciously minty scent released into the air.

"And it's supposed to help with aches and pains? Smells good enough to eat."

"I wouldn't." They both laughed.

The study door opened. The doctor walked inside, followed by Lucas, his shirt hanging open. Lucy cleared her throat and instinctively took a step back, away from Seth.

"Liam said you had that charmed poultice of Sophia's to put on Lucas's shoulder," the doctor said, looking at Lucy.

She glanced down at the canister she held and quickly returned the lid before handing it over. "I hear it's magical," she whispered with a polite smile. "If you'll excuse me, I think

Mara and Alex might need help in the kitchen." She turned to Seth. "Thank you for your help."

Lucas made no attempt to cover his exposed mid-section. Lucy had to force herself to look away. She'd seen plenty of shirtless men since coming to the ranch, but she hadn't been attracted to them the way she was to him. Heat rushed into her cheeks as she slipped from the room and headed for the kitchen.

Tillie was busy with Mara finalizing the preparations for the big Thanksgiving meal.

"Mr. Deardon isn't feeling very well today," Mara said, "but if I know Liam, he will still insist on helping the boys deliver the food crates to Mrs. Hamilton and the children."

Lucy sat down at the table where several delicious looking pies cooled in the window sill. Liam had been planning the trip to the orphanage since she'd arrived, making sure that there would be plenty of food and sweets to go around. He didn't do anything small. Everything was a grand gesture with him and she appreciated his efforts.

She'd only been sixteen when her mother had been taken from her. The holidays had never been the same after that. Until now.

DING! CLANG! DING! CLANG! DING!

"Alex must be ready to start the tournament. She loves ringing that dinner bell. Have you heard from Lucas?" Mara asked Lucy. "Is he still going to be able to compete?"

"He's in the study with the doctor," Lucy replied through a lump in her throat. The thought of his bared abdomen heated her cheeks. Again. She had to stop thinking about that man. At least for now.

"Why Lucy Russell, are you blushing?" Mara asked, wiping her hands on her apron. Scarcely taking her eyes off Lucy, she removed the protective garment and hung it from one of the knobs on the pantry cabinets.

"Why would I be blushing?"

"Oh, I don't know…only because every eligible man on this ranch is competing for your hand in marriage."

Lucy smiled.

"You'd better go tell the newest Deardon at Whisper Ridge that he'll lose his chance if he doesn't get outside." Mara exited the back door.

Lucy shook her head and made her way to the study, making sure to knock before pushing open the door. To her surprise, the room was empty, so she headed outside and over to the part of the yard where the archery targets had been set up on individual wooden easels at various distances. She was glad to see that Jake had already moved the chairs to the other side of the porch, but they were also empty.

It didn't take long to find Liam, standing with an arrow strung in a bow and aimed at one of the targets. Lucy leaned down with her elbows on the edge of the porch railing, watching all of the men familiarize themselves with the bows they would use to shoot and listening to their dialogue.

"Just breathe out when you release the arrow," Liam told Lucas as he released the string. The arrow hit the target at the lower edge of the center circle. "Not too bad for an old man like me, eh?"

Lucas beamed at him, the look of admiration transparent in his eyes.

Lucy was glad they had the opportunity to get to know one another again. She wondered what it had been like for Lucas to have believed his whole life that his grandfather had wanted nothing to do with him only to discover that the thing he had wanted most was to have a relationship with his grandsons.

She'd never had the opportunity to know her own grandparents, but liked to believe they would have been something like Liam Deardon.

"Archers, take your marks!"

CHAPTER EIGHTEEN

Lucas watched his grandfather with awe as he hit the target with ease. So many years had been wasted. He wished his brothers could be here and made a mental note to wire them. He probably should have done that already, but he had been completely taken off guard by the hospitality and warmth with which he had been welcomed, and then the storm had hit and he just hadn't thought about it until now..

"Archers, take your marks!" Aunt Alex stood on a podium that had been constructed against the house.

Granddad handed him the bow and turned to leave, but stopped just two steps in and clapped Lucas on the back with a nod and a smile. "I'm glad you're home," he said. The two of them stood at nearly the same height and Lucas met his eyes.

"Me too." He didn't dare say more.

Liam Deardon was much more than he could have ever expected and his love and words of encouragement touched Lucas deeply. He glanced up to see Lucy leaning against one of the porch posts watching them. Her light hair curled in cascades down her shoulders and her eyes were alight with the excitement from the day. He entertained the thought of what it would be like to hold her. To kiss her perfect little mouth.

Granddad smiled gruffly and followed Lucas's gaze. "She's a good woman, son. She'll need a good man by her side." He took a step toward the porch. "Now, show me what you can do," he called back over his shoulder as he walked toward the front stairs where Lucy waited for him.

She wove her arm through his, then glanced up, a closed smile softening her already beautiful face.

A good man, he echoed.

With a tip of his hat, he turned his attention back to the event at hand.

Nine targets sat in a line three feet apart about fifty yards distance from his position. Each competitor stood in front of their intended target awaiting the go ahead. Lucas lifted his arms and rotated them backward, surprised at the relief the white poultice Doc had rubbed into his shoulder offered. He wanted to take full advantage of the time he had without pain and hoped the numbing effect would last through the next three events.

He pulled an arrow from the quiver attached to the hay bale in front of him and placed it carefully into the bow.

"Gentlemen," Alex called, "shoot."

Thud. Thud. Thud.

The sound of arrows hitting their marks made a melodic rhythm. Lucas breathed in and closed his eyes as he pulled the string backward. When he opened his eyes, his focus blurred everything around him, keeping a clear line between him and his target. He exhaled slowly and released the shaft.

Thwak! The arrow struck its intended destination in the center circle of the target, though slightly below direct center and a bit to the left.

YES!

He tightened his grip on the handle of the bow and smiled to himself. His grandfather had seen that.

A good man. Was he a good man? Was he good enough for

a woman as kind and as lovely as Lucy?

He glanced up at the porch where his grandfather sat leaning back in the chair, his eyes closed, a slight curve of his lips resting on his face. Lucas narrowed his eyes, frozen momentarily to his spot as he watched for even the slightest change in movement. Granddad sat perfectly still. Something was wrong. Lucy looked up from Liam and met his eyes, tears trailing her flushed cheeks. She folded her lips together and shook her head.

The bow slipped from his fingers to the ground.

No! No! No!

His heart pumped fiercely, his ears blocking out all other sounds. He focused on the distance between him and his grandfather, everything else a blur around him as he rushed toward the porch, jumped up and over the railing, and then fell to his knees at his grandfather's feet. He lifted the man's hand, still warm to the touch, and glanced up at his face—his expression at peace.

No! He hadn't had nearly enough time with him. Lucas dropped his head into his grandfather's lap.

"No," he whispered as the tears began to flow.

CHAPTER NINETEEN

December 01, 1861

"The Lord giveth, and the Lord taketh away."

Lucy barely heard the words the preacher spoke as she stared at the heaping mound of dirt that concealed the body of the once stranger who had become family to her. She'd spent the better half of the morning collecting an armful of heather foliage and the cold resilient camellia blossoms from Sophia's winter garden and thought it only fitting to have them for Liam, here under the big oak tree. She still wondered how they could bloom amidst the snow.

The temperatures had dropped severely over the last few days. Those in attendance were wrapped in thick coats and woolen hats, but their faces were red from the cold and their breath near frozen as it touched the air.

"He is now reunited with his sweetheart, Sophia, and his grandson, Henry," the preacher continued.

The warm touch of flesh brushed against her hand. Startled, she glanced up to see Lucas, stoic and strong, face forward, looking out into the expanse of the Deardon property overlooking the grave. She slipped her hand into his to offer a moment's comfort, but he held it tight and didn't let go.

It felt so good, so right, that they were here together, grieving together for a man they both had barely known, but dearly loved. She leaned into him, gaining strength from his. It seemed so unfair that Lucas had just found his grandfather again only to have him ripped away so suddenly.

"Now, we'd like to hear a few words from Liam's family." The preacher looked at Sam and Hank, who both joined him in front of everyone and shook the man's hand.

"Dad would have been surprised to see so many of you here," Sam said with half a smile as he rubbed his hands together. "I wish our brother Gabe and our sister Leah could be here to see it."

Lucy glanced around. The whole settlement of Thistleberry had taken time away from their farms, ranches, and work in town to be here. There weren't many children present, but Lucy hadn't expected them to bring their youngsters out in this cold.

"He was gruff and stubborn, but always fair," Sam continued, "and I know that he enjoyed being a part of this community. It was his idea to provide a Thanksgiving feast each year to the Thistleberry orphanage," he nodded at Mrs. Hamilton, the orphanage proprietress, "and taught us that good fortune brings with it the responsibility of caring for those in less abundant circumstances. He taught us how to find the joy life has to offer and hold onto it."

Hank took a step forward. "He passed from this good earth doing what he loved—spending time with his friends and family on Thanksgiving Day." He brought his hands up to his mouth, blowing his hot breath to warm them. "He will always be in our hearts." Hank simply nodded at the preacher to conclude the service. Hank had been a man of few words ever since she'd known him. She wasn't sure why she would expect anything more now.

Lucas squeezed Lucy's hand, then released it as he stepped up to the grave and turned around to face everyone in attendance. "I know most of you don't know me," his cheeks and nose had a rosy glow—the only indication he felt the cold, "but my name is Lucas Deardon and I am Liam Deardon's grandson."

An awed murmur rolled over the crowd.

"Many of you may know Gabe. I am his son, and I feel it only appropriate that I say a few words on behalf of my father."

Lucy placed her hand at her chest and bit her lip. She knew this would be hard on him, but also knew it would be healing. A light wind picked up and Lucy rubbed her wool-covered arms against the chill.

"Death took my granddad from us unexpectedly, with so much still left to say and do. I have to admit that I feel a little cheated of the time me and my brothers spent separated from our Granddad. I only returned recently and was blessed enough to spend a few days with him before the Good Lord saw fit to take him, but in that time my eyes were opened to the goodness of his heart and the bond that family shares—no matter how long we've been apart."

He looked at Hank, but his uncle avoided his eyes and dropped his gaze to the ground.

"I know my father would be too stubborn to say it, but my brothers and I missed out on a great opportunity to get to know my granddad, to work alongside him, and to learn from him." He looked at Seth. "Whisper Ridge, and the people here," he looked directly at Lucy, "have become like home to me and I will miss them when I return to Oregon."

He's leaving?

"Thank you all for living as he taught…How did you put it, Uncle Sam? Caring for those in less abundant circumstances."

Sam nodded.

"I was a stranger and he took me in." Lucas paused. He clenched his jaw and swallowed hard. "You can't find a better example of living the Lord's teachings than that, Preacher."

The pastor held up his bible.

"Granddad taught me in a short time what I'd failed to learn in the past twenty some odd years—the importance of taking chances, and not just the kind that finds me bucked off a wild mustang with an injured shoulder."

Everyone laughed.

"He taught me to remember that life is only what you make of it," he said kicking at the ground, "and to…" he looked up at Hank, "…to forgive. Thank you." Lucas locked eyes with Lucy's and strode back to where she stood, scooping her hand into his, and led her to the opposite side of the grandiose oak, away from prying eyes and ears.

"I am taking one of those chances right now, Miss Lucy. With you," he whispered as he reached for her hand. "Granddad had it right all along and I couldn't see it, but somehow, he knew that you and I…that we…could create the most amazing life together. I know the tournament was supposed to determine your beau, but I don't want to leave it to chance. I don't want to wait anymore. Marry me, Lucy Russell. Be my wife."

She'd given up hope a long time ago that she would be able to marry for love. Her stepfather had touted her to the available men in New York as a good housekeeper, a cook, a washerwoman. But, she'd grown tired of caring for someone else's family and had wanted a family of her own.

Lucy wasn't silly enough to believe that what she felt for Lucas Deardon after a single week was perfect, but it *was* love—if only in the newest sense of the word. She loved him. In that moment, something changed inside of her. She saw her life in a new light. She'd come west with a promise of a new life and she'd found that—grateful it wasn't as Gilroy Hearn's mail-order bride. But she had to ask herself why Lucas wanted to marry her.

Now that Liam was gone, she felt a little lost and longed for his direction, his guidance.

"Mr. Deardon…I…"

"Ashes to ashes and dust to dust," the preacher's words were supposed to lead in to the music that would conclude the service.

The cathartic sound of bagpipes playing pulled Lucy's thoughts back to the wake. She slipped her hand from Lucas's.

"I have to go." She hurried to the edge of the graveside and looked out at many unknown and familiar faces alike, then glanced back over her shoulder to see Lucas standing there, his brows knit together, his face solemn.

Seth and Daniel moved to stand next to her as their bagpipes transitioned into the song they had rehearsed. The air went still, and for a brief moment, the sun warmed her unopposed.

"Amazing Grace, how sweet the sound…" she closed her eyes as she sang, allowing the words to fill her heart. "I once was lost, but now I'm found, was blind, but now, I see." She glanced back at the shadow of the tree.

Lucas was gone.

CHAPTER TWENTY

"A singer?" Lucas shoved his hands through his hair. "Real funny, Granddad."

Alone in his room, he sat down on the corner of the bed with a nice view of the oak tree out the window. He pushed open the glass and listened, despite the tremendous chill that whirled into his room. He pulled his coat up tighter around his neck.

"I once was lost and now I'm found…"

Lucas scoffed. He'd thought he'd been found, but right now he felt lost all over again.

He had to give it to her, Lucy's voice was like that of an angel's. He didn't remember much about his mother, but he could still hear the sound of her voice as she sang him to sleep. That voice that had brought so much comfort and then had caused so much pain.

He remembered a time, not too long ago, when Jonah struggled with the same thing. Lucas's own advice to his brother came back to him in perfect clarity.

Not every woman is going to be like mama, he'd told him. And at this moment, he sure hoped he was right.

Lucy finished up her song and bagpipes subsided—the only sound that followed was the creak of the swaying trees as the new breeze passed by. More than a few townsfolk wiped their eyes as one by one they stood and slowly made their way up to the house.

Several of the women from town and varying homesteads throughout the valley had worked together to provide a light luncheon for the folks who'd come to pay their respects. Lucas knew he should be out there greeting guests, thanking them, and introducing himself, but what was the point? He would just be leaving for Oregon in a few days and it wouldn't matter if anyone in Thistleberry remembered him.

Quit wallowing, Deardon.

Knock. Knock.

Lucas looked up to see Sam leaning against the frame of the open door.

"What you said out there was real nice, Lucas." His uncle stepped inside. "Brrr." He shook his shoulders. "It's freezing in here," he said as he crossed the room, closed the window, and then moved to sit next to him on the bed. "You must know how much it meant to your granddad to have you here. He was very proud of the man you've become. Couldn't stop talking about you the other night."

"I've been trying to understand why Dad kept us away from him. From Whisper Ridge. What was so horrible that he couldn't forgive? What drove him away?"

"That's not an easy answer, kid."

"Sure it is," Uncle Hank said in a matter-of-fact tone as he stepped into the room. "Your father didn't want to see the truth and in order to save his precious pride, he left."

"The truth about what?" Lucas looked at Hank.

His uncle scrubbed at his stubbled neck with the backs of his fingers, but did not answer immediately. "Maybe it's best you don't know."

"Best for who?"

"He's got a right to know, Henry."

It was the first time Lucas had ever heard anyone call his Uncle Hank by his given name.

"Let's just say that your mother had one foot out the door long before she left for Chicago."

"How'd you—"

"Your granddad told us."

Lucas stood and faced both of his uncles. "I am not a child anymore. You can tell me what happened. Why did we leave? What? Did my mother try to get a job singing here?" He couldn't imagine what was so hard to tell him.

What could possibly be that bad?

Hank stood up, threw his hands in the air, and stormed for the door. "Your mother tried to ruin everything. With Mara and me. She…She…" Hank shook his head.

"She crawled into Hank's bed one night while Mara was out of town visiting her mother," Sam finished for him. "But Mara came home early and found Lorna…in her bed. With a sleeping Hank."

"I can't listen to this again." Hank stomped out of the room.

"Hank went immediately and told your pa, but Gabe wouldn't listen. Wouldn't believe him. Couldn't believe that the mother of his children and the love of his life could have done such a thing. He chose to believe the yarn that Lorna'd spun for him, claiming that Hank tried to take advantage of her." Sam patted Lucas on the back. "They fought. Dad sided with Hank. Gabe left. End of story."

Lucas felt like he should be surprised at Sam's words, but somehow it all rang too true.

"But Mama walked out a long time ago. He had to have known what she was then. That Hank had been telling the truth. What kept him away after that?"

"Do you know your father at all?" Sam asked with a chuckle.

Lucas breathed a laugh. Gabe Deardon was a prideful man and his vanity had kept him separated from his family for the past fourteen years. Hell, it was what had separated all of them in the first place. Suddenly, Lucas felt sorry for his father. They had all missed out on so much. He dropped his head.

"I think it's time for me to go home." He sat up to look at his uncle.

Sam studied him, an undiscernible expression resting on his features. After a moment he nodded with a reassuring smile. "You are home, Lucas." And with that, he stood up and crossed the room, pausing at the door and turning back to look at him. "Dad's lawyer, Mr. Tacy, has called for a meeting so he can read the contents of your granddad's will. He wants to begin at noon. Join us in the main study. If you still want to leave after that, I won't stop you. But I might advise you to stay until spring. Wouldn't want you to freeze to death on the trail. It is winter, after all." His uncle bobbed his head. His pursed lips scrunched together as if he was trying to stop himself from saying more. With one last nod, he left, pulling the door closed behind him.

Reading Granddad's will?

Lucas had only known the man five minutes. How could anything in Liam Deardon's last testament make him stay?

Knock. Knock.

He glanced up, but when the door didn't open immediately, he pushed himself up off the bed and swung it open wide, half expecting Seth and Daniel to coax him downstairs.

"We need to talk." Lucy marched past him and into the room.

"Come on in," he said to the empty hall. He turned to look at her and immediately wished he hadn't. Her cheeks were flushed and her hair curled slightly, framing her face and falling in light disarray over her shoulders. Even with her arms folded and her lips absent of their natural curve, she was easily the most beautiful woman he had ever seen.

"A man does not just propose marriage to a woman and then walk away." Her chin raised as she turned slightly away from him.

"I'm not the one who walked away." Heaven help him, but he liked seeing her flustered and off kilter. It made her a little more vulnerable and, he guessed, that didn't happen very often.

"I'd made a prior commitment. To sing. At your grandfather's wake!" Her voice grew louder as she spoke, then softened eerily. "What did you expect me to do?"

"Answer." It was simple enough.

Lucy opened her mouth, then closed it again. She threw her arms up, her hands brushing the air before she dropped them to her sides. Her eyes flitted over his. "Mr. Deardon, I…"

Lucas closed the distance between them in a few purposeful strides.

"I think we're beyond the formalities, don't you? My name is Lucas."

She bit her lip.

He groaned.

"I understand that you agreed to sing for my grandfather's wake, and I feel bad that I didn't even know that you *could* sing, but I have to know something."

"Mr. Dear—" She put her hand up in front of her and closed her eyes. "Lucas, I…" she shook her head, her eyes unable to meet his.

He placed his crooked finger beneath her chin and lifted her face so he could see her clearly.

What are you doing, Deardon?

Alarm bells sounded in his head and he swallowed the lump that had formed in his throat. His heart pounded in his ears, his jaw flexed, and everything inside of him said he should step back, but he could not make himself pull his hand away from her.

"Tell me you don't want to get married." The intoxicating scent of citrus infused in her hair filled his nostrils as a light breeze worked through the house, blowing her tresses in wisps in front of him. "Tell me you dream of running away and singing on a big, fancy stage." He captured her hand and pinned it to his chest. "Tell me you don't think about me. Tell me you don't want me," he pleaded, "and I will leave for Oregon tomorrow and you will never see me again."

Painstaking silence.

"I can't tell you any of those things," she finally whispered.

Damn.

CHAPTER TWENTY-ONE

Lucy had come to Thistleberry, Montana, with every intention of marrying a perfect stranger, but she hadn't expected the turn of events that would lead her to fall in love with Lucas Deardon. She looked up into his eyes and knew she could never deny the feelings that had taken root deep inside of her. What was she afraid of?

He waited an answer, his hand gently caressing her jaw and skimming her bottom lip. Her gaze moved from his eyes to his mouth.

Oh, my goodness. He's going to kiss me.

The hand holding hers to his chest dropped to her waist, but she didn't move, reveling in the feel of his taut muscles beneath his fancy buttoned shirt. As he bent his head down toward her, her breath caught in her ribs and she closed her eyes.

"Lucas," a woman's voice called from his doorway, "have you seen Lu…"

Lucy jumped back, her fingertips shooting to her mouth, brushing her lips.

"Well, this makes everything so much more interesting."

Mara leaned against the doorframe with her arms folded across her chest and a smile that claimed to know more than there was to tell.

"What do you mean *more* interesting?" Lucas asked, narrowing his eyes at his aunt.

"I mean, Gilroy Hearn is downstairs in the parlor room waiting to speak with his mail-order bride. You know, the man she was supposed to marry."

Lucy didn't dare look at Lucas. She hadn't wanted him to find out this way. Not that there was much to tell. Liam had explained to her many times that her mail-order intended had run away with another woman and she was better off without the likes of him.

She hadn't understood his reasons at the time for why he'd felt responsible, but he had provided more than she could have dreamed—a roof over her head, food to eat, gainful employment with a fair wage, and most importantly, his friendship. It was now comforting to know that he had been such an important part of her family's history.

Gilroy Hearn?

What was the cowardly brute doing here now and what did he want with her? Didn't he have a bride he needed to be looking after? She stepped toward the door and stopped.

Gilroy Hearn, she repeated in her mind. The more she thought about him, the angrier she became. How dare the man show his face here after everything he'd done? She glanced into the mirror, pinched her cheeks, and squared her shoulders.

"I'll be right down." To her annoyance, her voice cracked as she slipped around Lucas and out the door, ready to give Mr. Hearn a piece of her mind.

"I hope you're not planning on letting her get away," she heard Mara tell Lucas before she nearly tripped down the stairs.

She'd left Lucas yet again without an answer.

Coward. Stop being so wishy-washy. She'd come west to get married and waiting for the man she loved to say the right words in return was just plain silly. Yet, she knew she needed to hear them.

When she walked into the parlor, a man of average height and mousy brown hair stood staring at one of the photographs on top of the piano, his hat in his hand behind his back.

"Hello," she called in greeting.

The man spun around to face her. "Miss Russell?" he asked, his brows raised and his voice higher than what she had expected.

"Yes, I am Lucy Russell. The mail-order bride you abandoned," she said matter-of-factly. "How can I help you, Mr. Hearn?"

The man was better looking than she had expected, but there was an air about him that put her on guard.

He rushed forward and collected her hands in his, shaking them both with eagerness. "Please, call me Roy. Forgive me for not being at the stage to meet you. I was otherwise…detained." He stood just a few inches taller than her, his hair was slicked back against his head, and a straggly line of whiskers, stretched thin above his lip, extended slightly beyond the width of his mouth.

"By a woman, I hear." She wanted to retrieve the words the moment they were out of her mouth. They sounded quite snippety. *Be polite*, she reminded herself, forcing a cordial smile.

His face fell slightly as he let go of her hands, his brows scrunched together. "I guess my mama *is* a woman. She's been real sick and needed someone to look after her."

It was Lucy's turn to scrunch her brows. "Your mama? It has been nearly six weeks, Mr. Hearn. How does your mother keep you away from your commitments for more than six weeks? Without as much as a word to the woman you had promised to marry?"

He twisted the hat in his hand, his head bowed, and he glanced up to meet her eyes. "I'm here now. Isn't that what's important?" He cleared his throat and craned his neck slightly to look at her. "And you are lovelier than I could have hoped. I know it's late, but I'm standing here, hoping you'll give me another chance."

The front door opened and Hank stepped inside the house, followed by Sam.

Mr. Hearn straightened his back and reached up to run a finger beneath his collar. He smiled nervously as he widened his stance, his gaze shifting from one Deardon to another. A slight curl in his lip twitched against a partially closed eye.

Mara joined her in the parlor and Lucy looked back to see Lucas descend the stairs. He paused, casually perching himself on the bottom step, and leaned against the railing. Hank and Sam stood on either side of the arched entryway into the parlor, folding their arms like sentries standing guard.

Mr. Hearn cleared his throat again, but looked at the ground. "Well, it's getting late yet. Maybe it's best I be going." He glanced up at her. "But I'll come back tomorrow to call on ya all proper like."

"Like hell you will," Hank said, one eyebrow raised. "You've got a lot of nerve, Hearn, showing your face around here again." He rested a hand over the holster on his hip. "The money you stole and used to pay Ardis Franks to tell her pa that you weren't the father of her baby, was meant for the orphanage. Children went to bed hungry every night for days before Dad found out what you'd done." He balled his free hand into a fist and then stretched it again.

Lucy's mouth dropped open at the blatant accusation, then turned her shock on Mr. Hearn. Hank was gruff and often discourteous to those who displeased him, but she'd never known him to lie.

A thief? And a cheat? How could she have been so naïve to believe that everything the man had written in his letters was true?

"Miss Russell, I assure you there is no truth to these outrageous charges," Mr. Hearn said with a slight bow of his head, as if pleading with her to believe him.

Hank took an intimidating step forward, but Mara rushed to him and placed a hand on her husband's arm. He looked down at her and took a deep breath.

"You are lucky my father thought a man—even a miscreant like you—should be given the chance to do the right thing."

"But now you've broken the arrangement," Sam spoke up. "Our father gave you enough money to marry the girl and start a small farm far away from Thistleberry on the condition that you promise never to return. So, what are you doing here?" He pushed himself away from the wall and took a step toward them, now standing even with Hank.

Mr. Hearn moved so that Lucy stood between him and the Deardon men, who effectively blocked his retreat.

"Now, hold on there, Deardon," Mr. Hearn said, peeking around her, "I come here to pay my respects to your pa. And while I was here, I thought I'd make things right with Miss Russell. There ain't nothing wrong with that."

"Except that we don't believe a word that comes out of your mouth," Sam countered.

"Don't you already have a wife?" Hank asked.

"Maybe you should mind your own business," Hearn said. His voice exposed a slight quiver. "Besides, shouldn't you be out there greetin' your visitors?" He pointed to the window with a tilt of his head.

"I think the boys can handle it for a few minutes," Hank replied. "And Lucy *is* our business."

She smiled at him with gratitude. It was nice having a family to look after her. And that is what they had become. Family.

"Funny thing," Sam said casually, "we did some digging around after you left and discovered that three of the colts you'd claimed had died from the last herd ended up on ranches in some of the neighboring towns. Very much alive. How do you think that happened?"

The tension in the room thickened and the silence grew. Lucy didn't want to be in the middle of the mounting confrontation.

"Lucas, why don't you go out and get the sheriff," Sam told his nephew. "I think he'll be real interested to hear what we've learned."

"You know what the penalty is in these parts for horse thievin'?" Hank asked.

Grateful the Deardons had forewent some of the more traditional mourning rituals they often displayed in New York society, Lucy caught a glimpse of Mr. Hearn in the large gilded mirror above the piano as he pulled a pistol tucked in the back of his pants.

"He's got a gun!" she yelled and tried to duck away, but he was too fast for her. As she jerked forward, his fingers curled into the long strands of her hair and he yanked her backward until she was close enough that he could slither an arm around her neck. He pulled her tight up against him, the stench of his hot breath searing her nostrils as he breathed hard against her ear.

"Nobody's going to be callin' on the sheriff today." Hearn spat as he waived the gun around, passing over each of them. When his aim finally settled on Lucas, he pulled back the hammer of his gun until it cocked. "Who the hell are you?"

Lucas appeared cool as could be as he turned to face her captor. "Lucas," he said as if that was enough.

"Well, don't you be trying anything funny over there, *Lucas*. I'll be leaving now, and Miss Russell will be coming with me." He turned to Hank. "Your pa done promised me a sizable dowry from this mail-order bride and I aim to take what's mine."

Dowry? She didn't have any dowry. What on earth could he be going on about?

"You've mis—"

"Shhhh," he cautioned, tightening his grip on her hair. "There'll be plenty of time for talking after the wedding." He sniggered.

"I'm afraid I can't let that happen."

The gravelly sound to Lucas's voice comforted Lucy and she glanced up at him, praying for his safety.

He met her eyes, his brow raised.

She nodded.

In one swift movement, he rolled off his perch against the railing and closed the few strides between them in an instant, his own gun drawn, the barrel of it resting up against Mr. Hearn's temple. "My grandfather entrusted me with Miss Russell's safekeeping. The only person she will be marrying, is me." He guided her away from Hearn's grasp and tucked her under his arm. "If she'll have me."

"Grandfather? Shoulda known you was one of 'em."

Sam rushed forward, slid the gun from Hearn's grasp, and gripped his shirt in a bunch just below the collar. "How could you have possibly believed that this was going to turn out in your favor?" he shook his head as he walked him toward the door.

Lucy turned into Lucas, wrapping her arms around his slender waist and squeezing, reveling in the feel of *his* arms as they encircled her with unexpected warmth and an unspoken promise of his protection.

"You're safe now," he said, then placed a gentle kiss atop her head.

"Thank you," she whispered against his chest.

After a moment, he pulled away from her enough that she could look up into his face.

"You still haven't answered me," he coaxed with some semblance of a smile.

She sucked in a deep breath.

You love him, idiot.

CHAPTER TWENTY-TWO

Lucas stared down into Lucy's eyes which reflected the rich grey hues of a coming storm as she looked up at him, her arms still encircled about his waist. The silence in the room was palpable and becoming increasingly uncomfortable.

"Why?" she whispered. "Why do you want to marry me?" she asked a little louder as her eyes flitted back and forth, searching his for an answer.

He hadn't expected the question and now felt slightly disconcerted as he searched for the right words, willing her to tell him what she needed to hear, but she remained quiet. Waiting.

"You are the kindest woman I have ever met. You are strong and beautiful, and I can't imagine my life without you."

There, he'd said it.

After a light twitch at the corners of her mouth, she offered a smile that warmed him from the inside.

"Yes, Mr. Deardon, I'll marry you," she finally uttered the words he'd needed to hear all day.

"Ahhhh," Mara said with a hand over her heart. "I thought you'd never get there."

He leaned down close to Lucy's ear. "Lucas," he reminded her, squeezing her close to him.

She smiled, something he hoped to see every day for the rest of his life.

"Lucas," she conceded.

"Congratulations, Lucas," Sam said, stepping forward, his hand extended.

"Thank you, sir. Sam. Uncle Sam?" Lucas was unsure how to address his uncle.

"Sam's fine."

Lucas looked down at his bride-to-be. He wanted to kiss her plump mouth. To taste the sweetness of her lips, but he was all too aware of their enquiring audience.

"What the hell were you thinking taking a chance like that with Lucy's life? And yours?" Hank didn't wait for a response. He marched to the front of the house, but turned back just before he left. "You are just like your father." The door slammed behind him.

"He didn't mean it like it sounded." Mara looked up at Lucas. "Gabe and Hank were closer than any two brothers I have ever seen. He misses your dad is all. And he just lost his own, God rest his soul. I expect he'll brood more than ever." She hugged both Lucas and Lucy. "Let's try not to dwell on what we've lost, but what we have to celebrate. A reuniting of Lucas with the family, Lucy coming here to live with us, and now the two of you finding each other. Liam would be so pleased that you've decided to marry. Somehow, he knew you would be a good match."

"He did, didn't he?" Lucy said as she turned out of his grasp and walked toward his aunt, a smile brushing across her mouth.

His arms suddenly felt empty.

"Yes." Mara grabbed Lucy's hand. "Now, let's go tell Alex. Let's tell everyone."

"But the timing. Won't people think us impertinent

sharing happy news? They will expect us to be in mourning. Maybe we should wait."

"Nonsense," Mara said, stopping at the door to retrieve their warm coats. "Everyone could use some good news today. And Liam, more than anyone, would want you to shout it from the rooftops just so he could say he'd told you so."

Lucy looked back at Lucas and shrugged before being whisked out through the front door.

It had only been a few days since he'd sent a message home about his grandfather's passing. A short telegraph message, however, could not possibly convey the sorrow and regret Lucas felt that his brothers had not been given the same opportunity to get to know the real Liam Deardon instead of the man their father had portrayed him to be their whole lives. He'd been good and kind and generous with his fortune. And had never stopped loving them.

Lucas had to find Seth. He had no idea how to work a telegraph machine, but wanted to send word to his family that he was getting married. He figured they'd want to hear something positive in spite of the tragic news.

Married.

He still could hardly believe it himself.

As he strode to the door, he caught glimpse of Lucy's smiling face through the window as Mara dragged her from one small group to another. His heart did a little flutter in his chest when she glanced back and caught him watching her.

He hadn't imagined he could ever feel this way about a woman, let alone one he'd only known such a short time, but even as his mind tried to convince him that he was marrying Lucy out of a sense of responsibility to fulfill his granddad's wishes, his heart knew otherwise.

He reached for the door, his shoulder stiff, but not painful like before, and when he pulled it open, the distinct smell of snow swirled about him.

Another storm's coming.

While the sky was still a vibrant blue, the air held a distinct chill as the sun started to play a game of hide and seek behind the growing number of ominous looking clouds. Lucas laughed at the irony. Today was both a sad and a happy day.

"I hear you, Granddad," he said with a breathy laugh as he ventured out to find his soon-to-be bride in the frosty morning air.

He didn't have to go far.

Lucy sat in the swing that dangled from one of the large trees at the edge of the main yard. Her arm wrapped around the rope and she leaned to the side, kicking her feet just enough that they brushed the ground as she swayed back and forth.

"A penny for your thoughts."

She looked up at him, a smile on her lips, but her wet eyes betrayed her. She brushed the tear from her cheek.

"I was just thinking about Liam. I miss him."

Lucas grabbed the rope of the swing and slowed it to a stop, then crouched down in front of her. "I miss him too."

"I didn't realize how much until Mara started telling everyone about our engagement. He was the first person who would have wanted to know." She laughed through her tears.

He stared at her for a moment, unsure how to best offer comfort. He reached out and placed a hand over hers. "He knows," he said confidently.

"Yes," she responded quietly, "I suppose he does."

Lucas leaned forward, his lips mere inches from hers.

Bark. Bark. Bark.

The large, beautiful border collie jumped up between him and Lucy and rested his paws in her lap.

She laughed.

"All right. Come on, boy! Let's get you some food." She looked up at him apologetically. "Sorry," she mouthed, then followed the barking dog toward the house.

He stood, unable to take his eyes off her retreating form.

"So, I understand congratulations are in order," Seth came up behind him and clapped him on the back, followed by several of his cousins as they circled about him.

Lucas watched Lucy until she disappeared into the house, then turned to face them.

"Granddad was right," Seth said with a wide smile. "You just needed a little push."

"A push for what?"

"Uh...nothing." Seth's eyes opened a little wider as he patted him again on the shoulder. "He just had a...um, a feeling about you and Lucy."

"I thought you *all* wanted the chance to marry Miss Russell." He looked at each of his cousins in the circle, recognizing that many of them were well under the marrying age. "If you thought granddad was right, why did you agree to compete for her hand?"

"Yeah, um...oh, I think Jake needs some help with all the horses from town." Seth turned on his heel and tapped the edge of his hat as he ran toward the barn, a grin spreading widely across his face.

Within seconds, all of his cousins had dispersed.

Odd. Then it hit him. It had been a ruse all along. *Smart man, Granddad.* He bobbed his head, not sure whether to be annoyed or impressed at his grandfather's ingenuity.

"I concede," he said aloud. "Lucy is most definitely the right woman for me."

The majority of those who had come to pay their respects to his grandfather had already headed for home, but a few hearty stragglers remained, making their way to the barn to retrieve their buckboards and horses.

A tall, gangly man, dressed in a fancy black suit and a matching bowler, caught Lucas's attention as he marched toward Hank. Lucas recognized the man as the lawyer he'd seen his first day at Whisper Ridge.

The will.

Hank pushed himself away from the fence he'd been leaning against and he and Sam headed indoors with the lawyer at their heels. Lucas reached inside of his thick winter coat and pulled his watch from the pocket of his vest. Quarter of twelve. They had just a few minutes.

As the sun broke out from behind a blanket of darkening clouds, it warmed the biting chill of the morning. The brief refuge from the unrelenting cold of the shadows quickly turned rival as the day darkened to a bitter grey. One lone snowflake drifted through the air, but he placed a hand on the top of his hat to keep it from falling and looked heavenward. Thousands of tiny crystals, glimmering in the low light, descended with increasing speed.

Lucas strode to the house, took the porch steps two at a time, and hurried inside. It appeared empty, but muffled voices reached him from the direction of the study. He hung his coat on the rack in the corner of the entry, but held onto his hat. It would give him something to do with his hands.

As he approached the study, he stopped at the sound of Lucy's voice.

"Thank you."

"I'm telling you, my dear, you should be on a big city stage. One of our associates is opening a theater in Denver and I think you would be just perfect. Folks would travel long distances to hear a voice like yours."

Lucas couldn't breathe.

No.

"That is very kind of you, Mr. Tacy..."

Lucas didn't hear the rest of their conversation. He needed air. He strode down the hallway and opened the door, but when the cool air hit his face, he stopped in his tracks.

Not every woman is like mama. NO! This stops now.

He turned around and marched back toward the study at a determined pace.

"If you, gentlemen, will just excuse me a moment..." Lucy

rounded the door of the study into the hallway. "I've been looking for—"

She didn't have time to finish before Lucas's hands delved into the hair at her nape, his fingertips guiding her head up to meet his kiss, his thumb caressing her jawline as his lips descended until they captured hers with hearty abandon.

She returned his affections, her arms wrapping beneath his and up his back to his shoulders, pulling him closer. He groaned. His hands dropped to her back, his fists clutching the material of her dress.

Easy, Deardon. It took him a moment before he garnered the will to stop. He pulled back, his eyes still closed, then with another quick peck of her lips he released her.

"Hello."

"I would like you to know, Miss Russell, that I think you *do* have a wonderful voice."

She glanced at the wall into the study. "You heard?"

He nodded.

"Well, thank you, *Mr. Deardon*, but you—"

"Having said that, I also need to tell you that I have seen too many misunderstandings and too much pride destroy too many lives for me to stay quiet. No matter what happens in there, I am in love with you, Lucy Russell. I…I just needed you to know."

"And I need *you* to know that what I said before is true. You asked me to tell you if I dreamed of singing on a fancy stage. I don't. You asked me to tell you that I don't think about or want you, but I do."

She leaned in closer to him and stood on her toes, so that her warm breath caressed his neck. "And I'll tell you what I told Mr. Tacy. I am not going anywhere…unless it is with you," she amended, "the man I want to spend the rest of my life with." She raised her hand and brushed it across his cheek. "I love you, Lucas Deardon."

Lucas kissed her firmly, then picked her up and spun her

around, reveling in the sound of her laughter.

"Are you two ready yet?" Sam asked, peeking his head out of the study.

They looked at each other and Lucas held out his hand. "No matter what happens?"

"No matter what happens," she affirmed.

"Let's go."

CHAPTER TWENTY-THREE

"Hank, wait,"

Sam called after his brother, who'd stormed from the study.

"Let him go," Mara said, placing a hand on Sam's arm, but Lucas couldn't do that.

He pushed himself up out of his chair, leaned down and kissed Lucy smack on the mouth, then grabbed his coat from the back of the chair and followed after his uncle.

When he got outside, Hank sat on the bench he'd carved and placed under the tree at the foot of his father's grave, his elbows resting on his knees, his hat in his hand. Lucas shoved his hands in his pockets and slowly made his way toward him. The thick snowflakes fell peacefully to the ground and it felt as if they had stepped into a bubble that silenced the rest of the world.

Lucas sat down next to Hank and leaned back against the bench.

"You are very talented. I've never seen craftsmanship like this before. It's beautiful."

"What do you want, Lucas?" Hank exhaled, his breath making small clouds in the cold air.

"I want to know why you hate me so much." The time for mincing words was over.

Hank looked up at him, then sat up straight.

"I don't hate you, Lucas." He paused for a long while. "Look, can we not do this right now?"

"I understand that you're upset." Lucas was still shocked at the generosity of his grandfather, and he understood how Hank might feel that his inheritance, and that of his father and brothers, was undeserving.

"Upset…Lucas. I just lost my father and I feel like I am losing my brother all over again. Yes, I'm upset." He threw himself against the back of the bench.

"I don't understand." How could he lose his brother again? He wasn't even here.

Hank pushed himself up and started to walk away.

"Help me understand, Uncle Hank." Lucas called to his uncle's retreating form. He rose too, but stood firmly rooted to the ground.

Hank stopped.

"Don't you need to get back to your ranch in Oregon? You got what you came for, right? Your inheritance." He took another step, then turned back again. "Oh, and don't worry, we'll pay you for the house."

"You know, despite what you said before, I'm not like my father, Hank. I am here! Right now. And I'm staying."

Clickity click.

"Not if I can help it."

Lucas whipped around in time to see Gilroy Hearn step out from behind the old oak tree, gun cocked.

Hank growled low in his throat. "How did you get away from Jeffers?"

Lucas stepped between his uncle and the jilted groom, but Hank came up quickly behind him.

"Now, you just stay put there, Hank." Hearn waved the gun Lucas suspected belonged to Sheriff Jeffers at Hank, motioning for him to stay back. "I wouldn't want nobody to get hurt. All I want is what your daddy promised me. You know, that girl's dowry. And then," he flung his hands haphazardly in the air, "I'll be on my way. Oh," he said as an afterthought, "after I kill this one, that is."

"Do you really want to add murder to your list of crimes?"

"Don't reckon it matters much now. Had you just let me marry the girl, none of this would have happened."

"The girl has a name," Lucas spat. "And she's too smart to end up with a hooligan like you."

"I know she's got a name. Miss Lucy Russell from New York City." He jerked his head to the side, preferably from the cold. "Now, just where is Miss Russell?"

Hank moved ever so slightly behind Lucas. He had to be pulling his gun.

"You might as well just toss it out right here where I can see it, Deardon. Lucas here got the drop on me once, but it's not going to happen again."

Hank tossed his gun out onto the snow.

"Hearn…" Hank paused. "Roy," he was going to try a different approach. "It might be difficult to give you Lucy's dowry. It's the main homestead here on Whisper Ridge. That's what she gets when she marries. I'm not so sure you'll be wanting that after today."

Gilroy rubbed his chin between his fingers, considering what Hank had told him.

"So, why don't I offer you a dozen horses and enough money to start over? Anywhere you like."

"You must take me for a fool, Deardon."

Lucas watched every flinch, every shiver, waiting for his moment.

"Not yet," Hank warned in a low whisper as he stepped past Lucas, his hands in the air, palms forward.

"Come on, Roy. Let's settle this like gentlemen."

"That's far enough." He reached into his back pocket, pulled out a set of handcuffs, and tossed them on the ground. "Pick 'em up. Real slow like."

Hank scrunched down to retrieve the restraints. "Where'd you get these, Roy? Where's the sheriff?"

"Let's just say Ol' Jeffers'll have quite a headache when he wakes up. Now, you sit down right over there on the ground next to that bench. You're gonna handcuff yourself to the leg."

"There's no need for that, Hearn." Lucas's jaw pulsed with constrained anger.

"I think there is. See, I take you down here and I'm a dead man." He looked back at Hank. "Go on."

Hank's eyes flitted to Lucas for a brief moment as he moved back toward the bench and he nodded.

Lucas chastised himself for leaving his gun next to his bed.

"Done," Hank called.

Gilroy flicked his wrist at Lucas, motioning toward the stable. "Turn around, *Lucas*. We're going for a little ride."

As they passed by the bench, with the gun still aimed at Lucas, Gilroy bent down to check that the handcuffs had been secured. Hank came at him with a large fallen branch and cocked him unsuspectingly in the jaw, sending the man sprawling backward.

Hearn recovered almost instantly, the gun still in his hand. "I warned you, Hank." He pointed the gun directly at his uncle, his finger squeezing the trigger.

"Stop!" Lucas screamed. "I'll go with you, willingly. Just leave him alone. You wanted me. You've got me."

CHAPTER TWENTY-FOUR

Gilroy walked up to Hank, still fighting to catch his breath, and landed a punch with his gunned hand in the jaw. Hank fell to the ground out cold.

Lucas breathed his momentary relief that Hank hadn't gotten himself shot. He looked at Hearn, his blood pumping fiercely through his veins, his temples pulsing violently, his teeth clenched.

Do something! Lucas scanned the yard, looking for anything he could use as leverage. Nothing.

Hearn closed the distance between them quickly, sticking the gun into the back of Lucas's ribs. "Want to try something else, hero?"

"Just take it easy, okay. What is it that you want from me?" he asked as they walked toward the stables.

"You said you were going to marry Lucy. She love you?"

"Yes."

"You love her?"

"Yes."

The door to the stables was open, which Lucas found odd with everyone gone into town for the afternoon. He looked down to see Jake, tied and gagged, slumped on the ground behind the tall work counter.

Snort. Whinny.

Adonis and one of the mares they'd used for the Thanksgiving Day race had been readied and tied to the front stall gate. Despite his madness, Gilroy Hearn was no idiot. Lucas looked for anything he could use as a weapon, but everything was just too far out of reach.

"Up ya go," he said, holding the gun higher, pointing to a saddled Adonis.

Hope filtered its way into the dire situation and Lucas mounted. Gilroy appeared to be an experienced rider, as he pulled himself up onto the mare's back, the aim of his gun never faltering.

"Easy now. We're going to cross the bridge and head off Deardon property to the south."

Lucas kissed the air and nudged Adonis forward.

"And, Lucas, don't try anything funny. I'd hate for anything to happen to that horse," Gilroy threatened.

Clomp. Clomp. The snow crunched beneath the horse's feet. Lucas waited until they reached the middle, then he squeezed his knees together signaling Adonis to rear. Lucas slid easily to the opposite side of the horse, effectively hiding himself from the brute. However, the action startled Gilroy's mare. Her feet slid on the newly frozen wood and she bucked Hearn off, sending a stray shot into the air.

Lucas pulled himself back up in time to see Hearn tumble from the edge of the bridge.

He closed his eyes with relief. "Whoa, boy," he called as he patted and rubbed Adonis's neck. "Good job."

The mare Hearn had been riding, stomped and pranced on the fresh snow piling up on the grassy bank at the base of the bridge. There was no time to collect her now, he needed to get back to uncle Hank to make sure he was all right. He pulled Adonis around.

BOOM!

Adonis reared again, and Lucas slid backward, but his hands tightened on the reins and he stayed mounted. When he gained control, he looked up to see Uncle Hank running toward him, a rifle in hand, and Gilroy Hearn lying face down in a rapidly forming pool of his own blood, gun outstretched, pointed toward him.

He could have killed me.

Lucas dismounted, his chest heaving with ragged breaths, his heart racing.

Hank barreled into him, grasping Lucas's body in his vice-like arms. He pounded Lucas's back a few times before he finally let him go.

"You said you're staying," he said as he sucked in a lungful of air, "and I'm going to hold you to that." He wrapped an arm around him and patted his shoulder as they started back across the bridge.

"Yes, sir."

"Let's start with you calling me Hank."

Lucy couldn't have imagined a more beautiful day surrounded by family and newfound friends. Whisper Ridge had been the perfect location for their wedding. She looked out of their bedroom window at the snow-covered ground, a frosty blanket of glittering diamonds and smiled. She was home.

Lucas came to stand behind her, his hands running down the length of her arms, then he wrapped her tightly in the warmth of his embrace as they stared together out at the old oak tree.

"Do you, Lucy Russell, promise to love me," Lucas kissed her on the side of the neck, "to cherish me," he trailed his kisses up to her ear, "and to honor me, all the days of thy life?"

he asked as he turned her to face him.

"I do," she replied, as she stared lovingly into the catch-lights of his mesmerizingly blue eyes. The moon's beams filled their bedroom with a soft winter's light that contrasted beautifully with the glow of the fire burning in the hearth.

"And do you, Lucas Samuel Deardon, promise to love *me*," she slipped her cool hands beneath the fabric of his open shirt and ran them up his bared chest, "to cherish me," she combed her fingers through the short hairs at the nape of his neck, "and to honor me, all the days of thy life?" She bit her lip and smiled.

"Forever, my love. And always."

"Then, *we*, Lucas Deardon, will always be happy together. We are home."

THE END

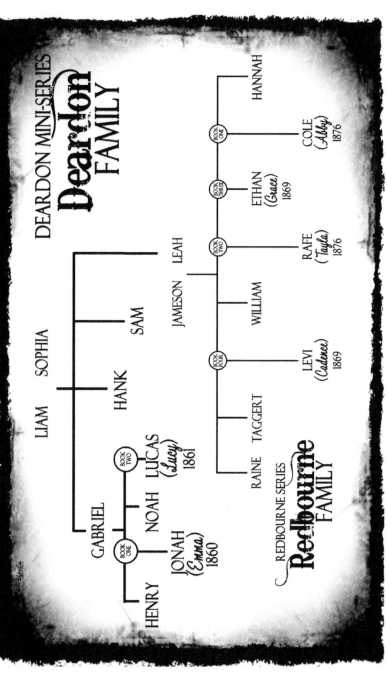

ABOUT THE AUTHOR

KELLI ANN MORGAN recognized a passion for writing at a very young age. Since that time, she has devoted herself to creativity of all sorts—moonlighting as a cover designer, photographer, jewelry designer, motivational speaker, and more.

She has been asked many times why she writes western historical romance novels and the answer is simple--she loves romance, chivalrous cowboys, horses, and the Old West. Love stories carry throughout the ages and she feels that it is important that when her readers curl up with a good book that he or she is transported into a world where the heroes always win. And when the ride is over, she hopes you'll feel uplifted, satisfied, and ready for the next adventure. Her novels are on the sensual side of PG—without all the graphic love scenes.

<u>www.kelliannmorgan.com</u>

WATCH FOR

NOAH

DEARDON MINI-SERIES, BOOK THREE

OTHER PG WESTERN READS
YOU MIGHT ENJOY...

KRISTIN HOLT
THE BRIDE LOTTERY

CAROLINE FYFFE
MONTANA DAWN

KIMBERLY KREY
CASSIE'S COWBOY CRAVE

BELLA BOWEN
GENEVIEVE

KIT MORGAN
AUGUST

DIANE DARCY
STEAL HIS HEART

Printed in Great Britain
by Amazon